A DEATH AT THE BAR

A DEATH AT THE BAR

by

CHARLES DRUMMOND, *pseud.*

(Kenneth Giles)

WALKER AND COMPANY
New York

First published in the United States of America in 1973
by the Walker Publishing Company, Inc.

ISBN: 0-8027-5259-4

Library of Congress Catalog Card Number: 72-80527

Printed in the United States of America.

1   2   3   4   5   6   7   8   9

CHAPTER ONE

IT WAS TEN days into the New Year and snowing at nine o'clock in the morning when Sergeant Reed, his red nose peeping between hat and turned-up overcoat collar, walked slowly along Lamb Lane in the City of London. He was on his way to a certain coffee shop where forgathered various men believed to be instrumental in doping greyhounds. It was purely routine, good for a morning away from Scotland Yard. The public houses, alas, were still shut, but Reed had fortified himself with a flask of brandy in his hip pocket and he was meditating a swift sip of the contents. Ahead, on a corner opposite a fur warehouse, was the Admiral Byng, named after the famous sea dog. A good City boozer, thought Reed approvingly, with excellent food, though it being under the authority of the City of London Police he rarely entered it.

As he neared, the big door opened and a small man rapidly emerged. Reed quickened his pace : the small man trotted towards him and Reed interposed his bulk. "Police here," he said, "what are *you* up to?"

"Joe Pollick," said the small man, "head barman. The boss is at the saloon bar with the back of his head stove in."

"Lead me!"

Last night's glasses had been cleaned and put away, but cigarette butts littered the floor. Leaning over the long, oak-veneered bar was a big man, his head down and horrible to look at. Reed reached out a cautious hand : the body was stiff.

"Get to the nearest phone box and call the police," he said.

The barman made off.

"Use your eyes," was the dictum of England's greatest

5

living forensic scientist—Reed remembered the lecture in which this gentleman had mentioned two officials who had omitted to notice a corpse brushed, as it were, under the carpet. He walked up and down the bar, looking. There seemed nothing out of place. He looked at the publican—Harry Alwyn, it had said in the statutory notice above the entrance. It might have been a bottle, but peering close Reed, from experience, thought it equally could have been a short piece of lead piping, wielded, say, half a dozen times.

Like a thirsty sailor on a raft at sea, the proximity to things he could not drink was torture to Reed.

"Wot's all this?" said a female basso. "Where's Mr. Pollick? 'Allo, wot's 'appened to his 'ead?"

"Police here. Sergeant Reed of the Yard."

She was an oldish lady in an ancient pair of men's slacks, a heavy duffel coat and a kind of cap.

"Mr. Pollick is out phoning from a call box: nothing must be touched here. Who are you?"

"Mrs. Crippen," she looked at him aggressively. "Mrs. Crippen wot has cleaned out both bars for nine years and then done the dining-room and kitchen, finishing at twelve o'clock, never before and never after."

"Know anything about this?"

" 'E was all right for a publican," said Mrs. Crippen, "never no trouble. 'E was fine, eating a piece of steak 'e was, when I left yesterday. I saw the back of 'is 'ead quite clear as I went out the door."

"You'd better knock off for today and turn up tomorrow."

Reed had time for a double tot of brandy from his flask before the police cars arrived. The local Inspector did not show much enthusiasm when he saw him, but later shrugged and said: "We'll be calling you people in, no doubt, so you had better do the reporting. It'll save time."

Joe Pollick glanced nervously at the corpse. The technicians and the police surgeon were beginning their gloomy chores. A pub was about the worst possible place to case, thought Reed, a mess of cigarette butts and fingerprints.

6

"What's upstairs?" asked the City Inspector.

"One floor," said Pollick. "A bathroom and the old billiards room Mr. Alwyn had made into a one-room flat for himself, plus some big storage cupboards."

"We'd better go up there. You, too, Mr. Reed."

A door from the snack bar opened on to a flight of carpeted stairs.

"That's the bathroom," said Pollick.

Reed peeked in. The plumbing was expensive and very modern. It smelled of bath oil. The late Harry Alwyn had obviously looked after his grooming.

The flat itself was basically a large room with one single bed, an alcove with a small sink, a two-burner electric stove, and various cupboards and bookshelves built in. A man could be comfortable there. There were several hundred books. Alwyn's taste had been catholic, practically everything was represented. There was a largish section on crime. The library had been sorted in an orderly way and the room had a kind of military neatness about it. The City Inspector had noted it, too.

"Who cleans this?"

"Let me begin at the beginning, sir. The bar staff is me and four barmaids, one part-time during the midday swill. Mr. Alwyn is—was—serving at lunchtime, too. There are three waitresses in the dining-room at midday and one behind the cold buffet. Chef comes in at ten and quits at five —in the evening there is only the buffet. He has three helpers in the kitchen, one working the washing-up machine. A Mrs. Crippen comes in at nine and I get here at five to nine to let her in."

"Why didn't Alwyn do it?"

"He did not sleep here very often," hesitated Pollick. "I'd say perhaps half the time only. It was difficult to tell unless I saw him come down those stairs, but after all it was none of my business. Then there are a couple of other cleaning women who come in at three to do out the place for the

7

evening trade, and one of them would 'do' the boss's bathroom and apartment."

"A big staff!"

"Not many pubs do our trade," said Pollick.

"Two bars, haven't you?"

"Saloon and public, plus a bottle department which is really an extension of the public and serviced by the barmaid on duty there."

The City Inspector had never been on licensing matters. He asked stolidly: "Can you give me an idea of the nature of the trade?"

"Lunches and snacks are the best value in London, sir. We're run off our feet between twelve and two and that's a gospel fact. Run off our trotters. Business men, of course, not many women, and the Corps of Commissionaires and suchlike in the public, where we serve a lunch over the counter, oxtail and the like, very filling. We are only tied to the brewery for beer, sir, and the Guv'nor used to have his own brands of wine and a house whisky, a bit cheaper than the supermarkets. A lot of people come here for them."

"Sounds a philanthropical type of landlord."

"You must make money on turnover, sir. And at nights I was often in charge. Nothing like midday, but very steady, very sweet. There are no parking problems at night, sir, the streets being dead and, begging your pardon I'm sure, not too many police around with breathalysers. So often people called in, Mr. Alwyn never stinting the heating in winter, for the best snacks in London and good drink."

"Where was Alwyn's other pad?"

"I don't know, sir. I always thought," Pollick's wrinkled face improbably succeeded in looking coy, "that there was a lady."

"Where is Mrs. Alwyn?" asked the City Inspector, the English licensing courts rather insisting on matrimony.

"I think the poor gentleman was no longer speaking to her. She had left him."

"Long hours for you," suggested the Inspector.

8

"I know the trade," said Pollick, "and I'm honest. When he took me on Mr. Alwyn said he did not mind what he paid for those two things. It's hard work but the money is there, that's what matters."

"We'll finish the routine," said the City Inspector to Reed who had sedulously taken notes. "It is Quant, isn't it, to whom you report?"

"Yes," said Reed, suddenly conscious of brandied breath and the City Inspector's disapproving glance.

"Give him the gist of it and tell him I'll come along around noon."

So in half an hour, by which time the pubs had opened, groaned Reed to himself, the Sergeant was tapping at the door of Chief Superintendent Quant's rosewood-lined office, currently lined also with rows of improper photographs upon which the old Super was preparing a report to the Home Secretary, subsequently to be delivered to a somnolent House of Parliament.

"It is to an extent a matter of angle," he was writing with his ancient, large-barrelled fountain pen when Reed's knock aroused him. No young and presumably lusty constable could be admitted, Quant's inborn Methodist conscience warned him, so he creaked erect and peered round the door, feeling relieved, the Sergeant's hobby notoriously being alcohol.

"Ugly lot, Mr. Quant," said the Sergeant casually.

"What God has made, Sergeant," said Quant with awful solemnity, being a lay preacher.

"Shall not be put asunder," said Reed, breathing brandy fumes and seating himself without ado.

Quant sighed. He put up with the Sergeant because of Reed's ruthless intelligence and what the Superintendent, though realising it was pagan, put down to luck. "Report what you have to, Sergeant," he groaned.

Reed pulled out his shorthand notebook and spoke for twenty minutes.

9

"What did ye think?" eventually asked Quant at his most Scottish.

"I didn't like the smell."

"A front for something? Women?"

"Improbable in a City pub, sir."

"Those?" The Superintendent's bony finger impaled the indecent photographs.

"Last briefing we had, sir, that business originates from the Mafia. I cannot imagine them operating a staid City of London pub. He just might have been the front for some of the clever boys who want to rack up a legitimate income-tax loss. If so we will find that he had formed a private company."

"It will come up at the five o'clock conference chaired by the Commander," said the old Super (why could he not be left in peace with these filthy pictures to complete this urgent report for Whitehall?). "So you had better be there."

Quant watched the door close and wearily gathered up his photographs. It struck him that there was no reason why they should festoon his office—they had made the old tea lady giggle to such an extent that she had slopped the fluid over on to the marie biscuits in the saucer : on the other hand he always found his reports were brighter if he was looking at actual evidence.

The Commander, a stout but agile-minded gentleman increasingly dissatisfied with his lot (he craved some minuscule but remaining colonial governorship in the tropics) had pre-digested Quant's four o'clock report. The big conference room included three Superintendents and six Inspectors. He watched with distaste 'that fellow Reed' tip-toe to a small desk at the back.

He turned on the loudspeaker system and ran through Quant's tape. Then he called upon Inspector Booker of Stolen Goods.

"Deceased was 'known'," said Booker, "as a fence."

"Why the devil did he get the licence?" snarled the Commander.

"No convictions, impeccable references, a Military Medal in the War, nothing against him. He had gone to a training school for six months to learn catering, plus one month as a barman in a hotel. The brewery company to which the pub is 'tied' liked him."

"Sounds as though the ingoing to the pub would cost plenty," said somebody.

"It did. He paid by cheque, that was ten years ago. Before that he ran a little tobacco shop out Brixton way, that was when the rumours reached us. He was, gentlemen, a 'foreign' fence. He handled stuff stolen on the Continent. You may not remember a jewellery theft in Tours in 1958. It amounted in our currency to thirty-eight thousand pounds. We heard he fenced that. He took and always has taken each year three two-week trips to Europe. The programme of disposing of stolen property, the small valuable items, has become international. The men and money to combat it do not exist. Therefore it is very difficult to prevent a moderate-carat diamond, of no special distinction and stolen in Rome, being sold here with little risk. The headquarters is Brussels. In the tourist season the continental Customs virtually cease to exist except for percentage checks and searching 'known' carriers. the *modus op.* is to use students as carriers—on cheap tours or in cars. Stolen jewellery moves about Europe almost at will. A lot of it goes by the Algeciras ferry to Tangiers— virtually no Customs control prevails.

"There is, of course, a market here. It is tied up with the 'black' money movements. The gems must be of perfect quality, but small enough not to be identifiable. The persons who fence them here are almost impossible to catch. Of course, if we raided them and discovered a quantity of stones we would demand an explanation, and failing it bring a theft charge, but with slim prospects of getting a jury to convict. The defence is inevitably that defendant took them as security on a loan to somebody who subsequently disappeared.

We believe that Alwyn did not keep stolen property at the public house : there were intermediaries."

"Alwyn had another residence," said the Commander, irritably watching the sleet hit the double-glazed window and thinking of nubile Polynesian ladies who disdained bras, "where was it?"

"We do not know," said the Inspector, aggressively. "Increase my staff three times and this sort of information I could provide."

('Economy must be our watchword', a very important person had ordered the unfortunate Commander that morning.)

Reed switched on his microphone. "Find the woman," he said.

"That does seem the pertinent point," said the Commander with distaste, in the direction of Quant, who bowed his bald head in a mixture of obedience and despair at the morals of the inhabitants of London.

"There are," said Inspector Booker, "thirty-four places in a standard-type car where things can be concealed. About the best way is to dent the bodywork, put the envelope of stones into it, fill with plastic filler and paint over. Theoretically the Customs have power to take a car to—literally— pieces. They have no obligation to put it together again," he gave a bureaucrat's chuckle. "But it is very rare that they assert that right. Thank God, gentlemen, people do not realise how easy and lucrative smuggling is. If I had my time over again . . . well, I might have been tempted. We believe that Alwyn was a Tempter, as we call them. Take a party of students in an old car going abroad. They meet a man in Brussels, Paris or Malaga, the conventional tourist beat, who buys them a drink. An interesting worldly man. After a recherché little dinner—he knows all the little off-beat places —he makes the proposition, say two hundred pounds in the local currency, the car to be borrowed overnight and put into a designated garage for a similar time in London. We know this because one lot of students would not play and reported to us as soon as they hit Dover. There was six thousand pounds' worth, retail, of stones set into the bodywork. There was no trace of the original owners, and the legal department still has it under study. They may well legally belong to the students who informed. The genial man who put up the proposition was probably Alwyn in a curly black wig and heavy, dark glasses, but there was no positive identification."

"How would the finance work?" asked the Commander.

"Take ten thousand pounds retail of stolen jewellery, the gold or platinum settings are taken off—no trouble about that stuff at all—leaving, say, nine thousand pounds' worth of stones. It is sold for two thousand pounds in Brussels. There would be a middle man who takes, say, five hundred as his profit plus the expenses. Alwyn would buy the loot for three thousand and sell it for five thousand, give or take ten per cent, in London."

"What would be his yearly profit?" asked Quant.

"Say, ten thousand a year clear after expenses."

Reed switched on his microphone. "The money must be somewhere and he must have had an objective. I mean that he would not want indefinitely to continue being a publican, not with ten thousand a year income-tax free."

"He was forty-seven," said the Commander. "Probably nearing retirement to some country with a bit of sun over it. He was an orphan, brought up by an uncle at Cheltenham. A bright lad, he won a scholarship to grammar school, went to the War and as a private got his decoration as the only survivor of a company which had been isolated for hours. He had injuries for which he got a five per cent pension. His accountant said that he made two thousand a year from the pub, gross, an abnormally low percentage. He obviously provided the best of everything, which adds up to a very skilled front. The more people who came in, the heavier his cover. And that is about where we stand at the moment."

"Anything else from the accountancy side?" queried Quant dismally.

"Nothing. He paid tax on approximately eighteen hundred pounds a year. His banking account, with the Midland, is divided into business and private. The figures are quite normal : his personal account stands at three hundred pounds. Therefore he must have had other ways of keeping his money. The banks or the Post Office Savings Bank have no knowledge of any other account in Alwyn's name. Of course in the criminal world, if you die suddenly your partner takes all the assets."

"Anybody inherit the pub?" asked Reed.

"At a preliminary check he died intestate. If there is a Will his accountant—who also dealt with the solicitor who did the conveyancing of the lease—knows nothing of it," said the Commander.

"I'm sorry to harp on it," said Reed, "but what of his wife?"

"There is no record that he ever was married, at least under the name of Harry Alwyn. He *was* Harry, by the way, and not Harold. Therefore he lied for the purposes of obtaining the licence. There was a woman, but obviously not his wife. She was around the pub for a few months only. She might have been employed for the purpose."

"They usually check the references pretty thoroughly," said Inspector Booker.

"I managed to locate the references he gave, four of 'em," growled the Commander. "One referred to 'Mr. and Mrs. Alwyn' in glowing terms. They *seemed* impressive references—oh, no blame attaches to the licensing authorities—but the fact is that of the four referees two subsequently went down for six and seven years respectively and the other two decided to quit this country for the good of their health, not quite enough proved against them for a prosecution."

Quant, a man who rather dreaded making decisions because of the inherent peril involved in doing so, groaned to himself. It was time for him to make a forceful suggestion before scuttling back in peace to his rude photographs. He looked at the ceiling for inspiration.

He switched on his microphone. "Women . . ."

"Sergeant Reed already dealt with *that*," interposed the Commander irritably.

"But the woman who posed as his wife," said Quant, at his smoothest. "There was one and the chances are she is still about. I suggest that Mr. Reed and a small squad, say two others junior in seniority, are deputed to investigate the point. Inspector Booker and his men can look into the stolen-goods angle."

Presently Sergeant Reed went in pursuit of a slightly junior colleague, known as 'Crying' Jarvis because of his ploy of using human miseries to get people talking. As usual the dismal man was arguing with an accountant, this time in connection with using a taxi to attend, as official observer, an exhumation.

"It would hardly be decent for the police to arrive at such a solemn occasion by bus," Jarvis was groaning.

"Nevertheless I can only pass public transport," said the accountant, equally dismal. "Let us see, by the shortest route it is twenty pence."

Reed happened to know that Jarvis had cadged a lift from a friend, so as always happened he was up on the business. He waited until the transaction had been completed and the coins disappeared into the stout purse which the Sergeant always carried. The only possible route to Jarvis' heart was via non-alcoholic beverages and free food, so Reed took him to the canteen and bought a plate of cream buns.

"I used to know Alwyn," said Jarvis, whose knowledge of London was unrivalled. "Two years ago somebody telephoned and said there had been a breaking and entry there. I got the work sheet and went out. A nice fellow, I thought. If I recall correctly it was onion soup, a prime steak, a bit of plum tart and some cheese to follow, all on the house and no bill. It was a false alarm."

"Strange!"

"Strange?" said Jarvis, a man of no imaginative powers.

Reed would have pursued the subject, but for the approach of an eager beaver in the shape of one of the youngest sergeants by the name of Humphrey, a very lucky young man.*

Jarvis, who did not like people under thirty, stared at him with disapproval.

"Are you fellows on the murder?"

"You bloody well know we are," said Jarvis, "or you would not have come sidling up."

Humphrey flashed his white teeth. He was difficult to snub. "Could I join you?" he asked Reed. "I'm not on anything today, but if I do not look pretty sharp Mr. Quant is going to get me on to feelthy pictures, which is worse than death—all those little photographers with thick spectacles."

'Crying' Jarvis looked at Reed, as bound to by the stout Sergeant's two years' seniority. Reed was considering. All white choppers and aquiline features, curly black hair and blue eyes, Humphrey had considerable sex appeal and in the *cherchez-la-femme* business this was sometimes an asset. Jarvis excelled in his knowledge of female ailments, a certain key to the confidence of many elderly ladies—nobody could talk more comfortingly about pains in the knees than Jarvis. He himself could wheedle out information over a 'convivial glass'.

"We might need a sex maniac," he said, "so come along. Are you filled in?"

"I listened to the broadcast from the conference room."

It is the custom for conferences to be broadcast. In the bigger general offices you listen to them with half an ear, but sometimes an unsuspected coin drops.

"We had better start at the pub. It's closed, but the head barman is still there. Ten years ago is a long time," said Reed.

* *The Odds on Death* (Gollancz).

16

"Old customers?" asked Jarvis.

"Few regulars last ten years. They retire, change their jobs, just plain die or quarrel with somebody and don't come in any more," said Reed with expertise. "Humphrey, you go down and do the paper work. Mr. Jarvis and I will see about the car."

When they got to the Admiral Byng a pencilled notice on the door said 'Closed', to the puzzlement of some twenty people studying the phenomenon.

"They ain't allowed to close," said a red-faced man. "The law says they ain't—wot is justice comin' to, where are our rights a-going? Wot's George Brown going to do about the pubs closing like this? The police are in it. Corruption in 'igh places, that's for certain."

"Now," said Sergeant Jarvis, an old hand at dispelling crowds and affrays, "why not totter along to the next boozer and not cause a public nuisance?" His elbow expertly caught the red-faced man in the kidneys, rendering him temporarily speechless.

"Why should we 'ave to walk?" said a wizened char-woman. "With the public transport closing down like it is it's walk, walk if you're a member of the working class. I'd like to see wot Stayline would have done. Wot, close the boozers? 'e'd 'ave said! And half a dozen coppers would have been put agin the wall and shot. We want more liberty and Teddy 'Eath should use his iron hand like Stayline did."

"I must say," a dapper man hawed, "and speaking as a solicitor's clerk, they have no right to close during licensed hours. There is statutory obligation there. I shall take it up with my Member."

"A statuary obligation," said the charwoman, ominously. "It'll be seven years for the beer bung."

"Now, my old dear," said the Sergeant raising his voice. "We must be reverent in the presence of the Great Reaper."

"Who's been raped?" asked somebody avidly.

"Mr. Alwyn has been murdered," shouted Jarvis, "his head stove in. A sight to freeze the blood."

"Is the corpus still there?" asked the charwoman practically. "'E wasn't a bad old stick and I wouldn't mind doing the layin' out at rock-bottom price, it being a side-line so to speak."

"He is in the morgue," said Jarvis. "Now ladies and gents, if your heads was stove in, you would want the police to have a free hand to find the man who done it."

"They shouldn't have abandoned 'anging," said the charwoman. "The workin' class 'ave no protection. I shiver in my shoes on lonely streets."

"So," roared Jarvis, "you will show respect for Mr. Alwyn by moving along to the next boozer and giving us a free hand."

Reluctantly they dispersed, the red-faced man lurching in the rear.

"The public-bar lot," said Jarvis contemptuously, knocking at the door of the Admiral Byng. There was no reaction.

Sergeant Humphrey, conscious of the authority invested in Her Majesty's officers, applied his boot and a judas window slid open.

"Eff off," said the voice of Joe Pollick, "we're closed by the police."

"I *am* the police," said Humphrey.

"You look more like a pox doctor's clurk to me," grumbled Pollick.

"Now," said Reed, "you remember me from this morning!"

"'S right," said Pollick grudgingly and the door bolts grated back.

The corridor to the saloon was brightly lit as was the bar itself. "Mr. Pudding from the brewery is taking an inventory," said Pollick, who looked tired.

Mr. Pudding, who had the air of a man perpetually attached to a notebook, was amiable.

"He was only tied to us for beers, you know," he said, "so we are doing this as part of our well-known Brewery Follow-

Up Service. As soon as you are dead we take a complete inventory. It gains us a lot of good will."

"So I should imagine," said Reed. "Did you know Alwyn?"

"I was the first person in The Brewery"—Pudding spoke as of the Holy Grail—"to interview him, ten years ago, I suppose it was. A charming man who had taken pains to learn the job. Running a pub ain't all hay, you know."

Reed, from long experience, spotted a faint redness upon Mr. Pudding's face proceeding from a patina of small broken veins, and a tendency to lick his upper lip as if it were dry.

"Shall you be long?" he enquired.

"Just finishing up." Mr. Pudding's small, moist eyes looked at the Sergeant shrewdly.

"I suppose you met Mrs. Alwyn?"

"Eloise was a lovely lady, kind of gracious, like. But not for a pub," Mr. Pudding wagged his wise head. "Not for a pub. She didn't like getting her hands wet, I would say. And of course if they want to run off, they have so many opportunities. A strong character, powerful muscles, a face like the back of a bus and a tremendous bosom is what a publican needs in his wife, plus knowledge of cooking. Otherwise if it's not the customers it's the biscuit salesmen, a randy lot. Eloise lasted a year, then one day when I came in to collect the monthly account Harry told me she had scarpered. Sometimes they like to talk about it, but Harry was otherwise. It's a funny thing . . ."

"What is?"

"I saw her two months ago in a pub in Shadwell. Not owned by The Brewery, but doing well in an arty-crafty sort of way. Fashionable! So my Guv'nor said 'Pudding! Get down there and see what makes it tick'. It was about eight at night and there was a jolly crowd, difficult to place but I saw some theatricals out of a show enjoying themselves for the evening. Quite a few gays of the quieter type. Anyway it's a big boozer as they come, and as I said before very arty, very *avant*. There are some pictures hanging up marked twenty-five nicker each that I defy you to identify. A sudden boom that will finish as quick as it has begun. What they like is fake 1870 for the long road."

"What is the pub named?" asked Reed.

"Oh, yes, the Limping Man, a big old barn of a place dating from Gawd only knows when."

"And you saw Eloise?" persisted Reed.

"In a party down the end of the bar, about ten of 'em, some kind of celebration because they were on the champers. You couldn't miss her, about five feet eight, slim as a wand, and that kind of golden-red hair which makes them look as if they were going to float away. Hallo, hallo," he added, "we're missin' on a bottle of Chartreuse! Where's it gone, Mr. Pollick? We can't have Chartreuse, green and all, flying off."

"It was there yesterday," said Pollick tiredly. "Perhaps one of the ladies put it under the counter."

"It's not there," said Pudding testily. "All right, let it go until tomorrow. I'll let myself out. You'd better go home and open up as usual in the morning, the legal angle will have been covered. The Brewery will be sending somebody to help you with the catering worries."

"I tell you what," said Reed, glancing at all the bottles and casks lying defenceless like an Istanbul harem with the eunuchs fled, "I have work to do here. Oh, everything routine has been done, but I might do worse than poke around. Meantime, you, Mr. Jarvis, might take the car and Mr. Humphrey and have a look at this pub named the Limping Man. If I remember it was once a smugglers' place. They used to bring stuff up the Thames in thick fog as late as the nineteen twenties."

Jarvis hesitated, being of sufficient seniority to enter a caveat against any unreasonable order from Reed. Then he thought of the perks. It is very difficult for the most vigorous accountant in Victoria Street (and there are many) to positively disprove that a man has spent ten pounds when on duty upon licensed premises. There is supper money, late-night money and, if shrewdly worked, allowances for shoe leather. On all these counts 'Crying' Jarvis was a past practitioner, and upon this bait Reed had shrewdly gambled. As for young Humphrey, he plainly found the atmosphere of the Admiral Byng frankly oppressive and the thought of bright lights and brightish—one always hoped—girls more attractive.

"All right," said Jarvis, figuring that if he could not net seven pounds, he had indeed lost his touch. "Come on, Mr. Humphrey."

The pub was more silent than ever when Jarvis and Humphrey had gone, let out by Joe Pollick.

"I'll tell you what," said Mr. Pudding unnecessarily, "the keg beer isn't doing itself any good just sitting there. Supposing we have a generous gargle—on The Brewery, o' course."

"Pints, I dare say," said Joe Pollick slipping behind the bar and attending like a smallish major domo to his healing apparatus.

"A shade too much gas, Joe," opined Mr. Pudding when they were comfortably immersed in their fourth. "The Brewery is much against over-gassing."

"They ought to have my job," said Pollick, himself a silent quaffer. "I work my days in a sea of it. You look over the old counter and see them working their bottom jaws out. All lies, at that."

"Are you married, Mr. Pollick?" asked Reed.

"You're jokin'! Attract even more gas! No, Sergeant, me and a quiet little lady have a mutual arrangement, like. For eighteen years she was married to a barrister who used to rehearse his speeches in front of her. She now appreciates silence."

"We might now wash it down with a small whisky," suggested Mr. Pudding, "as I see that I inadvertently neglected to place that one there," his finger stabbed the air, "upon the inventory, and a very nice brand too."

"What about the soda?" asked Pollick. "Is that on your inventory?"

"The Brewery does not bother about soda," said Pudding with a certain magnificence.

"Nothing like a whisky upon beer," said Reed comfortably, sensing a trifle of alcoholic hostility in the air.

"I espied some savoury-looking viands upon the snack-bar counter," said Mr. Pudding, oblivious to insult. "Left over from last night, but the serving counter is refrigerated."

"I'll cope," said Reed. "Three mixed platefuls, no good letting it go bad."

The snack bar was in what had once been a passage to a store-room and bore the faintly ruined look that such places have after a heavy evening. There were the remains of a once noble veal-and-ham pie and depleted bowls of *hors d'œuvres*, but—Reed brightened—a plentiful supply of shaven smoked salmon. There was a flap in the counter and he pulled it to one side and went in to fill three platefuls.

"Russian muck," said Mr. Pudding presently, his red nostrils quivering as he scowled at the smoked salmon.

"You are thinking of caviar," suggested Reed.

"All the same," said Pudding, loudly relishing the veal-and-ham pie.

It certainly soaked up the beer, thought Reed who the fourth pint had bloated. He said so.

"The Brewery does not approve, sir," declaimed Mr. Pudding, "the Computers having proved that fresh, empty stomachs are what the industry needs. A slab of this, now," he speared the veal-and-ham, "means point four less intake of fluid per hour, equivalent to three per cent on shareholders' funds employed. It could be the ruin of the country, sir, The Brewery owning so much of it."

"Shall I get you a cab, Mr. Pudding?" asked Joe Pollick later.

"I have to do my duty," announced Mr. Pudding, with

the slightest list to starboard. "To wit our other fourteen houses in the vicinity, The Brewery being pretty thick around here. I shall inspect them, sir, greet each licensee so that he knows the Friendly Eye of The Brewery is upon him."

"It didn't save Mr. Alwyn from getting his head bashed in," said Pollick, sourly.

"That was after hours," said Mr. Pudding firmly, "The Brewery not being responsible for after hours. Did I have a hat?"

The resourceful Pollick produced a somewhat dusty bowler, and Mr. Pudding, apparently forgetting the Sergeant's existence, was escorted to the door. It did not seem to be a bad job at all, ruminated Reed. One could surely get the hang of the inventory business if Mr. Pudding could and The Brewery might jump at the chance of getting an experienced ex-C.I.D. sergeant as one of their district visitors. Of late Sergeant Reed had been increasingly aware of his unpopularity among the hierarchy. He became conscious of noises 'off'.

"Now, Mr. Bustard, we're closed because of the unhappy event to Mr. Alwyn's head," Joe Pollick was saying. "Yes, the police, or one of them, are here, but why can't you go to the local station like a Christian? Oh well!"

Reed hastily swallowed the whisky he had poured. The visitor was about five feet ten and built like a coffee table, prematurely bald with bright blue eyes. He was dressed rather smartly.

"Inspector?" he said.

"Sergeant Reed, C.I.D."

"I'm Bill Bustard. Here's my card."

The pasteboard slip said 'Bustard Brothers. If it's movable we'll move it', with an address at Knightsbridge.

"Perhaps we might move a whisky," suggested Reed.

"The better kind of removal and no breakages," said Bustard. Reed rather liked him. A Cockney by his accent, and Reed had learned not to trust them completely, owing to their inborn dislike of the police. You could still hear the old terms 'peeler' and 'copper' around the various 'manors'.

"Mr. Bustard was an old friend of Mr. Alwyn," said Joe Pollick as he poured.

"So he came round for a Wake," commented Reed dryly.

Bustard had the kind of skin which flushes easily and did so now. "It's true that he bought it last night? I mean the newspapers being inaccurate."

"About one," said Reed, "perhaps killed by a bottle or maybe a bit of piping. Dead immediately."

"I knew him for years," said Bustard. "He was a friend in a manner of speakin'. I'd like to see the bleeder that done it in maximum security."

"Boys together?" asked Reed. "Same school?"

"Lord no. I left Central School at fifteen to push a barrow. Harry came from the West Country—an orphan, his folk dying when he was eleven. There was a little bit of money and an old uncle. He went to grammar school and said that he was in line for the university, though I admit you had to take what he said with a grain of salt. I met him in the war, same company, and we got very friendly. You know how it can be."

"Very thick?"

"He was educated and read books, a beer and a bit of fun being more my line, but we were close, Sergeant. I know London, every rat-hole of it"—he stated it as a fact—"the good and the bad. Harry would listen to me for hours. Insatiable for information he was, and what a memory!"

"Look, Mr. Bustard, *why* are you here?"

"Difficult to say, really. I said that I'd like to see whoever did it put inside for life. Harry was a friend of mine. *But . . .*" he drained the whisky and Reed signalled to Joe Pollick to refill.

"I don't want you fellows to get on the wrong track," said Bustard. "Smooth, pretty well educated, what's the word? Urbane! No, the real Harry Alwyn was a twister. I've known too many of them to be mistaken, without having been pretty close to him at times."

"He appears to have had a pretty good war record," grunted Reed. "Wound up a lieutenant and got the M.M."

"Christ, we used to laugh about that one," said Bustard. "Harry wasn't going to have his head shot off for nobody, a lot of the lads felt that way though sometimes you had no control over your destiny. But Harry knew all the ropes and could bluff a doctor like nobody's business. He was trying to gasbag himself out on to civvy street with a bit of a pension. Mind you he was just about twenty years of age, and *they* spotted it. But the jerries were folding up when we got out there, and Harry worked it out that with a bit of whizz-work he'd come through O.K. but then the silly German bleeders did the Ardennes caper. Harry thought of shooting himself through the foot but the corporal kept an eye on him. He got sent out on a seven-man patrol, a lieutenant, a sergeant and five others. They walked right into it, a German patrol with maybe thirty men. Trust us to have too little too late. The lieutenant told Harry to cover them from the left flank. He crawled away and there in a ditch was a burnt-out tank. Harry got in and stayed there flat on his face listening to the fire. The rest of the boys held out for three hours until the last of them bought it.

"Night came and there was still a lot of activity, bombs falling around and Harry scared that some daft man would mistake the ruined tank for a live one and beat it up. He finally decided to get out and try to find somebody to give himself up to. He kept his rifle, but cut his ear badly getting out of the thing. You know how an ear bleeds! He was blinking around in the dark when the advancing Americans came across him, all blood, with his rifle in his hands and his dead comrades around. Cor! If there had been a surviving witness he might have got the V.C.! As it was they gave him the Military Medal. Harry complained about internal injuries and they flew him home for observation. He magged that out for two months, then got sent to an officers' training camp before the war finished. What a boy! I'd lost touch, but what happened was that he was stationed in Berlin for ten months and got in on the fake Leica camera racket. They looked like the real thing until you tried to take a photo. The lenses were made from old beer bottles. One day I'm walking down the Old Kent Road and there, nicely dressed, is old Harry strutting along. We have a drink and a giggle. He had a little tobacconist shop, you know the kind of place in those days, dirty little old shop with a forty-watt bulb without a shade."

"Did you think he made a living out of it?"

Bill Bustard laughed, but without much humour. "He spent as much on his lunch as the shop would make in two days, and at that it was quite often closed. Harry collected people, if you know what I mean. He was the kind of cove who had an address book listing everybody he had ever met with details of what they did. I reckoned I was just a drink for old times' sake stuff, but I mentioned I was working for my two brothers in the moving business. It's not only household effects but small, valuable parcels for certain firms. We've got a thief-proof van for that. I could see his ears cock. It doesn't pay badly so I struck while the iron was hot and told him I wanted to buy a partnership but hadn't got the fifteen hundred quid.

"We had several lunches," said Bustard, "and one day he just looked at me and said he'd lend me the cash for three years at three per cent real interest per year, better of course than I could ever have done elsewhere even if anyone had been interested. I'd been in and out of bank managers' offices until my feet wore out, and the money boys merely wanted all the profits. I took it, an agreement drawn up right and shipshape. To cut things short I worked on the smell of an oil rag and he got his dough in under three-and-a-half years. Thanks, I *will* have another."

"I suspect there was a *but* about it," said Reed softly.

"He used to throw work in my line—he knew a lot of people. The money I put into the company was used to buy equipment and we could handle most moving jobs. There was a small warehouse for short-term storage. Then there was work for him. Very small jobs to be done personally by yours truly. Packets or small leather cases discreetly collected and delivered. Oh, I never saw anybody except some old lady who handed me the goods or received them. It was mostly rooming houses or the type of flatlet you can rent for a week."

"You didn't feel impelled to see the local police sergeant?"

"For what? We're registered as common carriers with a bloody great list of regulations. Blood oozing out of the trunk, ominous tickings from the suitcase and it's our bounden duty to call the police. Otherwise we just take the money and move it. We're an honest firm, just ask around the trade."

"How long did this go on for?" asked Reed.

"Until I finished the repayment of the money. Then I said, 'Look Harry, boy, if you are strapped and it's an emergency call on me for old times' sake, but now take the carrying caper somewhere else.' He gave the old smile and said, 'You'll never get the M.M., Bill.' I said, 'I'll never get no ten years inside either.' He laughed with me, poor old sod. A year later he took this pub. We'd lost touch, what with me working like a ferret in a rabbit plague, but one day he phoned me up. Would I care to have a noggin with him at his pub? I did and I s'pose I used to come in here twice a week, sometimes for lunch, sometimes for a drink around eight at night, the warehouse being only a couple of miles away. It was strictly old times' sake. I think he needed an old friend, people do."

It was amazing, thought Reed, his eye on the nearly empty bottle, how much homely philosophy you got chucked at you during the course of the job.

"I don't reckon that old bleeder, Pudding, will notice another gone," said Joe Pollick, calmly opening a bottle, "and if he does he'll fake the figures."

"No more jobs for him?" The Sergeant addressed Bill Bustard.

"No. It developed into a kinda formal friendship, memories of twenty-five years ago sort of stuff. Once he said that the secret of his business was never staying on the same bit of ground too long."

"And what was his business?" snapped Reed.

"You are the tec. Stolen or smuggled goods, wouldn't you think?"

"Any idea of his partners?"

"I keep out of things like that. In the removing game you often meet up with Funny Business. The rule is to know nothing. My business is on the up-and-up, you can check with my accountant."

"Did he have a wife?"

"When he first took over the pub he did, not that I knew her except for 'Hallo Mrs. Alwyn!' A tall reddish-haired lady, slim and a bit stand-offish. Harry didn't talk about her. She had something, I dunno how to put it, which didn't quite ring true." He ruminated into his glass. "Lookin' back across the years she might have been an actress some time. They get a kind of affected manner after a few years on the boards, not quite normal, always striving after some kind of atmosphere so that it becomes a second nature, if you follow me."

"I suppose you knew her, Mr. Pollick?" asked Reed.

"You stay away from the Governor's wife," said Joe. "They have their ideas and the head barman has his. Never shall the twain meet. You get some annoying bitches in the trade, but she and I had an understanding. She did the food and I looked after the bar. It didn't last. One day she wasn't here. Alwyn wasn't much of a talker to the staff. He just told me to engage a lady to take over the food side, which I did. Only thing I can say is that the wife knew food, not arty-farty looking down a French menu, but good practical pub grub such as knowing how much meat you should cook on a Friday."

"Sounds a capable lady."

"Foodwise she was."

"Mr. Pudding seemed to think she might have been familiar with the bar customers."

"That old fool can only see the nearest bottle and I don't mean a titty-bottle. She could chatter away, anybody used to being the wrong side of the bar learns to do it without giving any offence. If you sense trouble in the air you polish a glass, stare a bit over their heads and don't say a word. She quickly cottoned on to that. I'd say with my experience of women that she was a coldish fish."

"And Harry Alwyn was not?"

"I'd say, and it should be a fiver for an expert witness's opinion, that he liked the ladies but kept it under control. Never touch the stock is a good pub motto, so we might as well have another, the exception proving the rule. Then I'm going home : it's freezing outside."

"When exactly was your last job for Alwyn?" Reed asked Bustard.

Bustard shuffled a little. "I told you that I gave up working for Harry eleven years ago almost, but I don't want to conceal anything. Three months ago he asked me to move a trunk, said it was urgent. He told me that he had been storing it for an old lady who wanted it in a hurry. I came one Thursday morning at eight thirty. Harry was waiting at the door. I helped him shift it downstairs from his little flat— only the third time, I guess, that I'd been up there. It was not heavy, but one of the old-time clumsy tin ones that cut your hands if you are not careful."

"You had transport?"

"A small van, the same one that I've got outside now. It was a block of flats, oldish 'uns, down near Kennington Oval. No lift, but it was the ground floor so I could cope. There was an old lady with thick glasses and dyed hair who was obviously waiting for the furniture to be delivered."

"Where was it?"

"I could find it, Sergeant, for I've got that kind of a mind, but the name and address has clean gone from my head."

It was ten thirty, Reed noted with something of a shock.

Joe Pollick was pointedly turning off the lights. "I have absolutely no right to ask you this, but could you drive me there?"

"Might as well," said Bustard good-humouredly.

"About time you did something else but booze," said Pollick.

"Can't I drop you?" asked Bustard.

"I live six minutes away. It's not worth it, besides which I'll clean up a little. You heard Pudding say that we'll open for business tomorrow morning. What a life! And when's the funeral? I should go."

"Probably a week," replied Reed. "After the Inquest, which won't be for a few days."

"I'll shut the front door behind you."

The snow had turned unpleasantly to slush that tended to slop on to the instep. They got into Bill Bustard's small van and turned up the heating. Bustard drove with the deceptive casualness of a professional.

"The old lady you delivered the trunk to," said Reed, "did you ever see her before?"

"Not to my knowledge. About five feet four, black dress, blond hair and steel glasses. It was all over in ten minutes. I just lugged the tin trunk into one of the empty rooms. She said, 'Oh, Mr. Alwyn is such a kind man. How much do I owe you?' I told her that Harry was footing the bill, though as it happens I didn't put one in. That was all."

"No cups of tea and little rock cakes?"

"I reckoned the flat was empty and she was waiting for her furniture to arrive."

Reed sat silently thinking. There are a lot of elderly ladies, retired after a life of crime, who make a little extra 'fronting'. Done properly, it is more or less foolproof, for juries are notoriously reluctant to convict old ladies, even those with a record. The cosy old soul who ostensibly owned the 'drop' for drugs or the dubious accommodation address could earn a few pounds with impunity if she was clever, and a lifetime of shoplifting or 'telling the story' was inclined to hone the wits. Reed knew quite a few of them, one a great-grand-mother with a total of around two hundred years of penal servitude in the family.

The block of flats, probably twenty in number, dated from the early twenties, thought Reed. They went through the swing door into the unheated, tiled corridor. "Second on the left," said Bustard without hesitation.

Reed rang the bell. After five minutes the door opened and a wave of heat flushed out. "Come in whoever you are," said a burly man in a long red brushed-nylon dressing-gown and bare feet, "I'm paying for this heat."

"Police," said Reed, producing his warrant card, which the burly man barely glanced at as he led them into a plea-santly furnished lounge room, marred by dull, brownish wallpaper.

"Sit down," he said. "Being such a beastly night the wife and I retired early with some books."

"Were you here three months ago?"

"No. We came in on November the first, back from our honeymoon."

"The place had been empty?"

"Two or three months, so I understood. I'll give you the name of the agent."

The burly man's name proved to be Satchard and he was a deputy advertising manager on a group of technical maga-zines. About twenty-seven, Reed thought. He said the flats were due for demolition in exactly nine months' time, which suited him nicely because at that date he was due to replace the retiring manager for Scotland. They were centrally heated and cheap because of the circumstances. Neither he nor his wife had elderly female relatives who visited them. There were some elderly people but they visited them as they had all retired to various places in the country.

"Sure you haven't made a mistake?" questioned Reed as he walked with Bustard back to the van.

"A thousand to one against," said the remover, "because

I've got that type of memory. Names I sometimes forget, places never or nearly so."

"Just drop me at the tube station," said Reed, looking at his watch. He thought of a bedtime hour in his little study enjoying the warmth and a couple of drinks. It was time to call it a day, and he wondered vaguely how Jarvis and Humphrey were making out.

In fact a strange series of circumstances had precipitated Sergeant Humphrey, amid the wreckage of a ruined single bed, into being accused of cuckolding his host, a large man with an inflamed look about him. The wife, a rather massive brunette, was endeavouring to pound her husband's head with a quart bottle of Spanish bath salts, while Sergeant Jarvis was intoning that he represented the Law in those parts.

It had started at the Limping Man which, as Mr. Pudding had done his best to indicate, was advanced in its decor and, if you could have used the word nowadays without getting into a fight, decidedly, determinedly gay.

Jarvis had discreetly parked the car. You could smell the strange odour of the Thames when snow has fallen, as though the greasy black mud is fighting to spread its presence through the sleety mess. The Limping Man was a low-slung building, with the accretions of time. Dr. Johnson had been fond of its oysters and salmon in the days when the bar was in fact a kind of little room in which presided the landlord and his wife. Inside it was crowded. Sergeant Humphrey, whose girl friend was on the arty side, was being educated in such matters and rather liked, or persuaded himself that he did, the paintings for sale hung around the walls. Jarvis sucked his teeth and groaned.

"Toothache!" commiserated the barman.

"Something cruel," swiftly said the Sergeant. "Perhaps a little drop of peppermint with a dash of lemonade to rinse it out with. I reckon it's the cold that makes the stoppings pop out."

"That's what happens to the mother-in-law," said the barman, "and her hearing aid packs up which don't improve her temper. And you, sir?"

Sergeant Humphrey absently ordered a small whisky, rather wishing he had Reed's capacity for absorption. Everyone seemed to know each other in the Limping Man: groups met, coalesced for twenty minutes, then re-integrated. He was on his second whisky, Jarvis opting for a dry ginger on account of certain ulcers, the condition of which he was willing to discuss avidly with the barman, when Humphrey became conscious of a slight pressure upon his toe cap. Not for the first time he was envious of the old timers' capacity to absorb and mentally file detail. The barman had moved away, serving champagne cocktails to a group of very merry people.

"With six people at the extreme end of the bar," muttered Jarvis. "Ethereal reddish blonde, the pre-Raphaelite type, no tits but wistful." In his queer way the dismal Sergeant was a mine of bits and pieces of knowledge.

"My God, but you could be right."

"Keep your voice down and don't goggle, my lad."

"I know her," said Humphrey, hurriedly staring down into his drink. "Either her or her double. One Melusina Drago who does modelling, which is how I met her through my girl friend. About thirty-five and does cabaret work when she can or occasionally musicals. Not bad but not quite good enough, the sort that makes a precarious living. Only thing I know is that she has a sense of humour."

Evidently Sergeant Jarvis did not approve of women having such senses because he looked more depressed than ever. "Make yourself known, if necessary I'd better be your uncle from Plymouth."

Come to think of it, thought Humphrey, Jarvis did stand out a little among this company, in his worn but respectable serge suit and the blue striped shirt with detachable collar

33

and cuffs, though he did really look like an uncle from Plymouth.

"In the grocery line," he suggested.

"Suits me. And a widower, the women liking widowers to talk to."

"Hallo!" said Humphrey after walking to the far end of the bar. "I saw you there: it's the first time I have ever been in here."

"It's just a habit," said Melusina Drago. "You'd better meet people. Let's see, you're John Humphrey..."

There were nine of them now, including a host, a red-faced man palpably with money and a statuesque brunette wife answering to 'June'.

"It's the lady's birthday," said the red-faced man, pinching June with gusto where it does ladies the most good. "Sixteen this morning, wasn't it, love?"

"I was never good at fractions," said June, who had a portwine laugh.

"We called in here for a quick one," said the red-faced man, "on our way home to a party in exactly three-quarters of an hour. It's done by caterers so numbers aren't any object. Come along with us. Got a car?"

"Yes, but I'm out with my uncle and..."

"Out with his uncle! I've heard everything! Do you ever go out with Auntie?" The speaker was a saucy little redhead that the Sergeant had his eye on.

"I'm perverted," he said, "but he's a very respectable man in the grocery business at Plymouth."

"Is he anything like the sailors?" asked June with interest.

"He rowed a boat on the Serpentine one time: he got dizzy."

The red-faced man had turned out to be Reg Gaukroger and of testy nature. "Let's get going then. Mel, you go with John and direct him and his uncle."

Melusina looked amused as Humphrey introduced her to 'Crying' Jarvis. "You look rather like your nephew, Mr. Jarvis!"

"He's got his health, my dear, no worries about wet socks like I have. I wish I'd brought my galoshes."

Jarvis did the driving. Humphrey sat in the back with Melusina. "Let's see," she said, "you are a policeman, aren't you?"

"Policemen have their nights off and their moments."

"So your girl friend once told me."

"A shrewd, capable and observant lady. But who is Mr. Gaukroger?"

"He deals in things," said Melusina, "and is fabulously wealthy with no friends except a horse he rides week-ends at his place in Sussex. The food and drink will be fab."

Humphrey noticed she was nursing a bottle. "Is it bring your own?" he asked. "If so we'd better stop at a pub to stock me and uncle up."

"Gaukroger would be offended. Somebody back from Torremolinos brought me this monstrous jar of cheap Spanish bath salts. I've had 'em before and they smell of imitation flowers under a hot sun. So it struck me as a good idea to give them to June who will give them to her maid, no doubt. But it's a *gesture* that will impress Reg Gaukroger who feels terribly inferior because his father was a Labour Town Councillor, or so June says, and they are good for a superb dinner once a fortnight. I live on such things."

The Gaukrogers lived in a mountain of apartments in Wembley, having the penthouse, which was surrounded by Spanish-type open patios, serviced by a firm which in any kind of propitious weather, which this was not, provided a daily service of flowering pots.

"He has a man constantly clearing the snow away," confided Melusina as they went up in the private lift, the rest of the party, as a result perhaps on the one side of Mr. Gaukroger's ferocious impatience and on the other of Jarvis' disposition to snail-like progress with a view to sundry expenses accruing from overtime, having gone up fifteen minutes ago.

35

"I must say you are not a go-getter, Uncle Jarvis," Melusina had observed.

"Do you know what happens when anybody falls dead over the wheel?" demanded the Sergeant, at his most lugubrious. "You don't because the motor and aircraft firms hush it up. And there are pains that the National Health say is wind round the heart. But do I *know*?"

"I must warn you that Mr. Gaukroger's culinary tastes run on the windy side, people tending to levitate at the evening's close."

"I wear copper bracelets round the legs for rheumatism," said Jarvis, hamming it a trifle, "and I don't reckon you levitate with copper round the calves."

Humphrey, as usual in his rare experiences of them, was confused by Reg Gaukroger's butler who was wearing civilian dress, and tried to shake a hand which the butler gently disengaged, performing the same service for Humphrey's coat and hat. Jarvis, with more experience, ostentatiously transferred some small change from his overcoat to his suit pocket and hoped it would not be kept in a damp place because of mildew.

It was a large penthouse, now pandemonium. People seemed to be coming in droves. A large man named Mac insisted on telling Humphrey about a recent deal involving cement to Bremen out of which he seemed to have done well.

Jarvis soon latched on to two portly dowagers—relatives of his hostess, concluded Humphrey—and they had jointly sequestered a large tray of lobster patties, the while settling down to a spirited discussion upon stomach acidity in the mornings. They ogled Jarvis admiringly when he told an astonished waiter that he wished for plain tomato juice.

Somewhat larger than life, Reg Gaukroger wandered morosely about as a greeter, a half-consumed Scotch in his hand. Observing him out of the corner of his eye Humphrey, making polite and unheard responses, could not decide whether his host was really drinking or whether it was a kind of stage prop.

Eventually Humphrey became rid of his man, who espied a larger operator who was talking of his achievements in selling pig—Humhprey double-took for an instant until he realised it was pig-iron—to Formosa. By that time there was a certain coming and going. 'Dropping in to Gaukroger's' was obviously the done thing. Two Scotches, canapés and vol-au-vent and then on somewhere else. He could not see his hostess, but Jarvis' two dowagers had been joined by three younger ladies who fairly hung upon the Sergeant's gloomy words about the curing of varicose veins.

Weaving his way, warm light ale in hand—he was not going to get tight on this one, not with the ambition of being the youngest Inspector ever since 1888, when one was hurriedly appointed in error, it being thought he had arrested Jack the Ripper. (It turned out that the arrested man was not drunk but totally paralysed.) Humphrey wormed through the crowd, wishing to God that Gaukroger, obviously a hot-house plant, would turn his central heating down a notch or so.

Melusina Drago was a trifle tight on gin-and-tonic. For her colouring she used very light lipstick and this had worn off. She was steadily eating a vast plate of pork terrine.

"Hallo, copper," she said, "if I see a disapproving glance it is because I am stoking up for tomorrow."

"I find that a funny thing," said Humphrey, "however much you stoke, you are hungry at about eleven next day. Some kind of law or other."

"You sound like your uncle," she said. "I passed him and he was on about indigestion. If he *is* your uncle."

"A Plymouth grocer!"

"Who uses a London tailor for his overcoat? I had a look when the butler was divesting him."

"He has a mistress here, in fact several." Humphrey lied wildly.

"Christ!" Miss Drago ate steadily for ten minutes. Then: "However much I eat I don't gain a pound. And don't

37

exercise your erudition by mentioning pre-Raphaelite. I'm just skinny, not ethereal."

Humphrey lurched as a backside jabbed his. "Sorry," said a fat man.

"Could I have a word with you on one of the terraces?" whispered Humphrey to Melusina.

"My dear, I'd catch my death and your kidneys would never be the same after that piercing wind."

"It's still and calm out and if you notice the temperature has risen."

"Oh, God, get me a very light G. & T. and I'm yours for exactly four minutes, in howling weather upon Gaukroger's infernal patio. What an inferiority complex the man has! He's insanely jealous of his wife, by the way, which I always warn young men of."

Humphrey got her the drink. He noticed Gaukroger complaining petulantly to the butler about the ice supply.

Melusina finished her gin, almost at a gulp, and meekly accompanied Humphrey to the smallest patio, one protected by plastic overhead but still cold.

"Melusina," said Humphrey, "how well did you know Harry Alwyn?"

"It's bloody cold and I have no idea what you are talking about."

"He was killed last night, at his pub."

"I read something in the *Standard*. That is all I know."

"When did you last see him?"

"I am not going to stand here getting frozen while you ask inane, melodramatic questions!" She pulled away from his arm and was gone.

Evidently the slush had been swept away from the environs of the Gaukroger penthouse fairly recently because the fancy tiles, though wet, were cleared. Humphrey found his way to an outside parapet and gazed down through the splodges of light from the apartment windows to the misty illumination of road and pavement. There seemed to be incessant small explosions as car doors closed. He did not think he had been at his best with Melusina. Humphrey was under no illusions about his sex appeal, but how did you make it work for you? It seemed to him that it was more likely to involve you in the support of ten children than gain promotion to Superintendent. Come to think of it he did not know a Super with any sex appeal. Eventually the itching of the chilblain upon his right big toe recalled him from these dismal thoughts. Of long duration, appearing each winter with the brussels sprouts, this disability had survived every cure and nostrum that his mother could discover. A gentle, soothing scratch was the only relief, providing a strangely sensual interlude in the Sergeant's secret life.

He obviously could not scratch it here, there not being a chair in sight.

He re-entered the penthouse. It was thinning out and only Jarvis was still eating, watched with some fascination by the catering staff. Humphrey unobtrusively passed into the hallway. The loos were clearly labelled, but in the Sergeant's experience unsuitable for the removal of sock and shoe, involving as it did a cramped and precarious feat of balancing. He saw a door ajar, a dim glow of light escaping. Perhaps the dining-room. Ready to beat a shuffling, conciliatory muttering retreat Humphrey eased inwards the door and peered round. It was a huge bedroom, elaborately furnished in a style that he vaguely recognised as Georgian except that the beds were two in number and rather oversized for singles. Upon one of these the Sergeant placed his fourteen stone and, bending, whipped off shoe and sock, revelling in the anticipated delight to come.

"Do your feet hurt too, dear? I don't know what's come over the chiropractors these days. My man's afraid to cut like he used to."

With some trepidation Humphrey recognised his hostess. She was fairly drunk. "A good idea," she observed, "I'll take mine off, too."

With that she slumped down heavily beside Humphrey. There was a crunching, tearing sound and the wooden structure of the bed collapsed into bits, leaving the Sergeant and Mrs. Gaukroger seated upon the mattress and elegant coverings. Mrs. Gaukroger first goggled incredulously, then lapsed into laughter.

"Wot's this?" It was his host's voice, cleared of cultural pretensions by sheer rage.

"'Oring in my own 'ome," declaimed Gaukroger bitterly, "defiling my marriage bed, breaking a valuable Georgian antique wot I paid three hundred nicker for."

"You louse, you shocking old bleeder. My mum will fix you, you graftin' old devil." Mrs. June Gaukroger had squirmed to her feet with surprising alacrity. Sprawling there, Humphrey saw that she bore Melusina Drago's birthday present of Spanish bath salts and that with this she was preparing to club her better half. But a serge-covered arm deftly reached over her shoulder and Sergeant Jarvis, appearing through the door, appropriated it. Jarvis had earned his spurs in a notoriously tough division where the separating of husband and wife was a nightly chore.

"Police here, break it up."

"Look at him, the obscene naked animal." Bouncing with fury, Gaukroger pointed in the general direction of Humphrey's chilblain.

"Easing his poor feet. He's a policeman too," said Jarvis with magnificent calm, only marred by the smell of lobster canapés. "And the bed has termites in it, I can see the eggs from here."

"I'll kill that dealer," howled Gaukroger, turning even redder. Humphrey took the opportunity to get to his feet.

"There has been enough violence," said Jarvis. "You must realise that hundreds of people in this wicked city would relish the idea of police protection. There are four gangs in the area preying on wealthy people. What with the new economy measures it's difficult for us to look after everybody, and very hard when we pick out somebody important to receive abuse."

"Well," said Gaukroger, partially appeased, "there is some

valuable stuff around here, but of course there is the insurance."

"My jules," said Mrs. Gaukroger and her spouse gave her a hard look of warning.

"But what," persisted Mr. Gaukroger, recovering his form, "is the point of guarding a house without shoes on?"

"Diseases of the feet are an occupational hazard, sir, shocking sometimes and dealt with at our own clinic. Occasionally the agony forces us to ease them."

"I've got a corn myself," said Gaukroger, more calmly surveying the wood dust on his floor, "but I'm damned if I go around breaking bloody beds. I suppose I'll have to take his word for it that he was investigating and not disporting like. June, join your guests and look happy and radiant!"

"Wait till I get my mum alone," she said darkly and, surprisingly, her husband visibly blenched. Nevertheless she went out.

"We must be on our way," said Jarvis, "and I can say that I wish everybody was as public spirited as you, sir."

Squatting, Humphrey was trying to perform the difficult feat of putting on his sock. "Leave that bloody thing alone," said Jarvis, his powerful hand hauling at Humphrey's biceps. The Sergeant got to his feet, carrying shoe and sock, and sneaked out into the hallway, past Jarvis. The pretty little redhead he had noticed in the pub earlier was leaning against the convex bosom of a pallid young man with a lot of hair around his face.

"Why has that chap only one shoe?" she was piping as Humphrey went out the door. As they got out of the lift and he attempted to hop his way into the car, Humphrey, a mild hypochondriac thanks to his mother's tutelage, thought about gangrene setting in to his chilblain.

"You drive and for God's sake turn that heater up," said Jarvis as they relaxed in the front seat of the Humber, "and put your ruddy shoe on, man. I'd better report in, then we'll change seats and you dictate yours. Take an old man's advice and include the bit about the bed in case Gaukroger puts in a complaint."

Presently they changed seats and, in his turn, Humphrey took up the radio telephone. His training made it a simple matter until near the end. "Owing to the intense cold," he intoned, "I entered my host's bedroom"—a cunning ploy, he thought, to avoid mention of it also being his hostess's— "and removed sock and shoe with a view to inspecting a painful chilblain upon the big toe contracted in the line of duty. My hostess entered suddenly, she having trouble with *her* feet. She sat heavily on the bed where I was ensconced and it collapsed, being ridden with termites, as Sergeant Jarvis will witness. My host entered and was naturally perturbed at the ruin of his antique bed, but Sergeant Jarvis and I offered suitable explanations."

Not bad, thought Jarvis, he perhaps might make something of the boy. Presently he turned the car into the parking area. "We'll take a taxi between us," he said, "and you can drop me off." Overcome with gratitude as he was Humphrey did not like, when the time came, to dun for money. It was another sixty pence up for Jarvis.

CHAPTER TWO

At eleven the next morning the Commander had a list of fifteen outstanding felonies. However Harry Alwyn's death had attracted the attention of the press, as violence on licensed premises always did. It was page one, in spite of the paucity of the facts, and thus number one on the Commander's agenda. There had been some criticism, culled from disappointed customers, concerning the day's closure of the Admiral Byng, and the Commander had personally checked that it would open this morning, neither sudden death, ruinous taxes nor massive bureaucracy counting for much as long as John Bull had his lukewarm beer and prohibitive spirits.

His liver touched by the previous night's over-indulgence in lobster with almonds at his Whitehall Club, the Commander viewed the room with distaste. Those who in the final analysis guarded the fortunes and safety of the British public looked a shop-soiled lot in the watery morning light which streamed through the skylight. Old Quant, sepulchral as ever though digestively soothed by his breakfast of lightly steamed cod, was not on top form. Incredible industry lasting until three a.m. had got rid of the dirty photographs: but on his return to his desk at seven thirty he had been confronted with a dossier composed of complaints from Public Library Committees about suggestive books. Could Mr. Quant provide a little something ... Therefore at this hour he looked more skeletonised than ever, having something like forty-eight pounds of paper to digest. Then there was that fellow Reed, in a sixty-guinea suit—the Commander recognised the maker—hiding himself at the back of the room. In fact Reed, once home, had communed too long with the rum bottle in his little study, listening to tapes, and had breakfasted merely on soda water and Fernet Branca. However, will power had enabled him to arrive at eight o'clock and type his report on the battered old portable machine which he insisted on using. It had taken him an hour before he had sent it up to Quant, by then surrounded by piles of dubious books submitted to their Members of Parliament by Watch Committees, Purity Leagues and Aldermen who had power over public librarians. Quant had pushed them away, groaned as he usually did—not at Reed but at the world in general and drink and fornication in particular—and after reading the fifteen hundred words had re-routed them to the Commander. From that point it was duplicated and went to half a dozen other officers.

When the throat-clearing and cigarette-lighting had subsided, the Commander said: "This man, Bill Bustard, Mr. Reed, how much of what he said is true, do you think?"

Reed rose and turned on his microphone. "It all rang true to me. He seemed to me to be a hard-working chap in the removal business who did Harry Alwyn a favour three months ago by moving a tin trunk. It is a classic example of the removal of hot goods. One moment they are there but the next they are not. I doubt whether Alwyn very often kept stolen goods at the Admiral Byng, but this time he was stuck with something. It smells very strongly of fear and double-crossing."

"With your permission, Commander," Inspector Booker, fair and immaculate in a neat pin-stripe suit, cut in. "It just might fit the Liverpool bank robbery."

Everybody in the room was familiar with that. It had been a small branch, in fact all of eighty years old and originally built to service offices in what had been a pleasant, outlying suburb. Now, quite suddenly and almost unexpectedly, it had become a large business sector, abounding with mail-order firms, credit book-makers, hire-purchase companies and the headquarters of chain stores. The little, old bank had fairly burst at its seams. With the innate dislike that all English banks have for new business, the Di-

44

rectors dithered over the problem of constructing a suitable new building. Meantime the old building, the cisterns of the staff loos sounding like fiercely played harmoniums, somehow staggered along with grossly swollen staff and land-office business. Large sums in cash were often held. The delivery to and fro was by a professionally run armoured car, unassailable in its efficiency.

The weak link was the bank itself. There was a strong room built in the year 1929. It had reinforced ferro-concrete walls, lined with steel, and a massive door with two locks and a time lock. By some prescience of the then manager it was a large vault. The weakness lay in the floor, which had not been reinforced, and in the fact that the bank abutted a three-storeyed building which had housed a wholesale bookseller who had gone out of business a year before the robbery. With neatly forged references the robbers had taken the vacant building on a five-year lease, rent payable three months in advance. It was their alleged intention to open display rooms and a small hardware warehouse for the building trade, a cunning ploy because nobody questioned the heavyish equipment which they took in. There were three men as far as anybody could remember, all very hairy in the modern manner. "Possibly built-up shoes, padded shoulders, wigs, etcetera," said the official report. They had been as unobtrusive as it is possible to be and had worked slowly in the basement two feet at a time for ten days. They made little noise, but again nobody would be suspicious of building noises coming from a building so plainly in a state of transition. The house agent stopped his car once or twice and one of the men—there was always one of them to 'front the house'—jovially stated that the repairs to the stairs were coming along nicely. The agent had rubbed his hands at the prospect of getting some free work done on the place for it was not a repairing lease. The whole job had no doubt been set up by one of those ingenious entrepreneurs of crime who provide a blue-print for a fee but personally have nothing to do with its execution. The three men came through the floor of the vault at approximately midnight on Saturday. They were quite secure, for the vault was time-locked until eight a.m. on the following Monday. There was a night watchman, but he heard nothing, the vault being virtually sound-proof. The thieves leisurely packed away two hundred and fifty thousand pounds in notes, seventy thousand in negotiable securities, held for a customer, and thirty thousand pounds' worth of uncut diamonds, deposited by a local wholesale jeweller.

Though not original, it was a perfect crime, the criminals unobtrusively departing—so it was believed—in a small grey delivery van at six a.m. Great care had been exercised to leave no finger-prints, although about one thousand pounds' worth of equipment had been jettisoned, but this in turn proved originally to have been stolen and was a dead end. The local police had then countered with a shrewd move, causing the rumour to be circulated that a large percentage of the stolen notes had their numbers registered. Inevitably the diamonds had sunk without trace, probably smuggled to Asia, while the securities were judiciously peddled in South America, but the rumour about the notes, passed back by informers, was that they were adjudged 'hot', so hot that an unnamed receiver had bought the booty for fifteen thousand 'clean' pounds. Eventually the police pinpointed two cunning grafters who very possibly were part of the trio who did the actual robbery: both were technicians and both showed unexpected affluence for a time. Yet there was no evidence.

"It's been jobbed about a good deal," said Booker. "We got one story that the original fence thought himself lucky to turn three hundred pounds when he resold. The thought of twenty years inside is a powerful deterrent against touching it."

"The picture of Harry Alwyn does not look like one of a man who took chances," observed the Commander.

"I think," said Booker, "that he had reached the point of retirement. He must have been too shrewd an operator not to realise that the point comes where your luck simply runs out, however careful you might be. He must have had a good sum cached somewhere, say a hundred thousand or so, taking his rather heavy costs into consideration. So perhaps he planned a final coup, with fifty thousand profit as the end. The point is that Harry Alwyn knew the European ropes and now that the amount of currency allowed out for travellers has been extended there is more of a market for pound notes. There is a flourishing exchange in the Lebanon, for although sterling is less desirable than Swiss, German or U.S. currency it is still in demand if suitably discounted, say fifteen per cent. It is a specialist transaction and not many thieves here have the necessary knowledge—or languages, which reputedly Alwyn had. It might be, of course, that Alwyn had inside knowledge that no numbers of the notes had actually been kept, thus being one up on the game."

"But why kill Alwyn?" queried an old member of the Murder Squad. "If he was the boy who was going to get the money out what was the point of touching him?"

"Suppose," said Superintendent Quant, "he had received his share and then had the goods hi-jacked. It happens all the time and is a sure recipe for violence. Or it might have been that Alwyn did not pay over the purchase money, that also can involve killing. I think we can proceed on the assumption that even if it was not the bank-robbery loot it was something of a similar nature. We have twenty robberies on the current listing of over twenty thousand pounds where the proceeds have not been recovered in whole or in part. To my recollection there has been no violence among the receivers of stolen goods for six years, not since that case in Birmingham."

(An old fence who masqueraded as a dealer in old silver had had his ears cut off after he had sadly reneged on a payment.)

"Some of the international stuff can be pretty rough," said Booker, "the Belgian mob, for one, and the crowd operating out of Cordoba can be nasty if crossed. We made it too tough for them here so they deal via intermediaries, like

47

Alwyn. Although I do not understand how he could have double-crossed them. In the international trade it is cash on the barrel head. Here you might wait a bit for your money, if it is over, say, five thousand pounds, but in the export and import business there is no trust."

"Suppose that Alwyn was cute and sold them a tin trunk filled with bits of newspaper, the oldest trick in the world," said an Inspector. "He might have reckoned himself pretty safe. I know that there are killings in pubs down the East End, with not a witness who admits to seeing 'nuffing', God bless 'em, but it would be difficult in a staid City establishment filled with reputable citizens."

"Reed," said the Commander, "while you are poking around find out if his habits altered in the three months before his death, whether he went out so much, whether he was suspicious of strangers, you know the stuff."

"I don't know about pubs generally," said Reed, and somebody gave a suppressed titter, silenced by the Commander's look. "Oh, I know the bar side," said the Sergeant unabashed, "but I did notice that all the locks were about as expensive as you can get and had probably been put in within the previous six months, which might mean that there was danger about."

"Would it not be easy," suggested Quant distastefully, "for an ingenious person to conceal himself in the pub after closing time?"

"I think that is routine in public-house life," said Reed, who had once got himself locked in a spirits store under the impression that it was a urinal, "but a careful publican makes a check. There are not many places where one could be concealed. It is not so much because of possible larceny as because of people passing out cold and perhaps being in need of medical assistance. The plans," he nodded to the blackboard on which they were pinned, "show a commodious cellar of the old type, with the only approach through a trapdoor on the serving side of the public bar. In the old days, barrels were rolled through the door, under the bar and down a ramp into the cellar. Entrance was by ladder, and to get into it you would have to unbolt the trapdoor and clamber down, hardly a practical proposition for a murderer. I think that Alwyn let somebody in by appointment, through the front door, which is the only entrance. Easy enough because the street is as dead as two dodos after midnight. They talked at the far end of the saloon bar, probably with one light switched on. There was a bottle of green Chartreuse that seems to be missing. It might have been the murder weapon. I don't think Alwyn was a liqueur man : the barman would surely have mentioned it. Assuming that death occurred at one o'clock in the morning, it is an odd kind of a drink to have at what was probably a business discussion."

"A woman," intoned old Quant, "they liking the sweet sticky sort of drinks, or so I've been told. The Pastor says that they're everlastingly swigging away at cheap, sweet sherry while scamping their household duties with the machines they have now. My old mother used to be on her knees from morning to night, mostly working but when the occasion occurred praying. Not a drop ever passed her lips . . ."

"Yes, yes, Mr. Quant," interposed the Commander, well aware that a diet of pornography, plus a late night and nervous indigestion, aroused the Chief Superintendent, "my own mother was an abstainer." (A lie, because the good lady had been one of the finest judges of claret in the country and when she was not pursuing this she was running after foxes, otters, stags and, when hard up, hares. But it soothed Quant.)

"I think," said Reed, "that the immediate lead is the tin trunk and who it went to. I might take a look at that if you care."

It was a formula that the Commander recognised. Most policemen had their own informers, and sometimes, by tacit official consent, these remained private property. There was a closely guarded central list of those people who made an income, sometimes surprisingly good, from 'shopping' associates and this was open to any senior officer seeking information. On the other hand the individual contacts were not trespassed upon. The quality of the informers was varied and sometimes surprising, ranging, in Sergeant Reed's case, from a counter hand in a fish-and-chip shop in Shoreditch, who was down on expenses for sixty pounds per year, to the butler of a Cabinet Minister, who informed not for money but from a sense of power and a temperament of general malevolence.

"You have a free hand within limits," the Commander said carefully. He thought he knew Reed.

"No lead to any woman in his life," said Quant petulantly. In the books he had been reading in the line of duty the women were all too readily apparent. "We must find the lady."

"If you please, Commander," said Jarvis, "I may have a slight lead on that. At the Gaukrogers' home I met some ladies, one being Gaukroger's mother-in-law who has bad varicose veins."

The Commander groped for the small blue pill which crashed down his blood pressure and made a resolution that there should be no salt or fluids for lunch.

Impervious to atmosphere as usual, the Sergeant continued. "Harry Alwyn was known there. One of the ladies mentioned him and they all fluttered. Such a nice man! What terrible news! When did you see him last, dear? One of the nastier ladies said, 'I see that poor June is bearing up wonderfully.' June is Mrs. Gaukroger and there was an embarrassed little silence. The old lady, though she's not that old, around fifty-eight or so but dresses very staid, was not amused. She is Cockney, but I would say one of the shrewd ones. Wears some very nice jewellery indeed. I thought—my nose told me—that Mrs. Gaukroger was Harry Alwyn's girl friend. She was getting high on gin: I did not pick her as a heavy drinker. There were no physical signs, and there was a certain amateurishness about her toping"— Jarvis could not forbear a side glance at Reed, who smiled placidly around the red pimples on his nose—"that was apparent. I would imagine that she drinks very little in the normal course of events. The old mother was keeping a steady eye on her."

"I got a report on Gaukroger," sighed the Commander. It had involved an outside Commercial Enquiry Agency specialising in the ramifications of credit and their fee would have to be explained by the Commander at his monthly audit. "He is a wheeler-dealer in a fairly big way, mostly in bankrupt and fire stocks. Pays cash and turns it over, working on a narrow margin. Not known to us, but apparently at one time he was an accountant, on his own in a small way. He married the present Mrs. Gaukroger eight years ago. Gaukroger is forty-eight, she thirty according to the marriage certificate. Nothing known about her family." The Commander hesitated. In the old days before the obligatory tape-recordings he could have said straight out that an old friend connected with Internal Revenue had told him *sub rosa* that one Reginald Gaukroger aroused some curiosity on account of spending some three thousand pounds per year on domestic expenditure—with typical thoroughness even the milk bills had been investigated—plus two thousand five hundred pounds per year rent—on a returned income of three thousand pounds. Mr. Gaukroger's able chartered accountant claimed that his unfortunate client lived in part off capital. Now he considered it wise to say into his microphone : "His financial affairs seem a trifle mysterious," and was rewarded by knowing leers.

"I hardly think," said the Commander, "that Gaukroger comes into this matter. His dealing seems strictly in the way of household goods on a large scale. Last week he apparently purchased fifty thousand blankets from the War Office. God knows why the War Office should spend its time buying goods which are subsequently flogged at half price through the classified advertisement columns! Anyway he'll make two thousand gross reselling them in packets of five thousand. That's the way he works, quick turnovers. If his wife was having an interlude with Alwyn, it probably doesn't mean much. There is nothing much we can do except tout her friends."

"One of the ladies, sir," said Jarvis, "invited me to have tea with her, she being a total abstainer and interested in a recipe I have to stimulate the skin, made out of herbs from the hedgerows." Like certain actors Jarvis got an unctuous, faintly perverted relish from guying himself. "This afternoon at four, sir! I thought I might persuade her to visit a cinema." This Jarvis had no intention of doing, having abandoned the cinema the instant he had paid his first television licence fee under pressure from his wife. But he had paved the way, including 'light refreshments', to a possible three pounds on the expenses. "She is a garrulous old biddy," said Jarvis, "and very sanctimonious. If there is dirt about Mrs. June Gaukroger, she'll spill it."

"Excellent," said the Commander. You had to pursue every lead: in fact he thought that the solution, if forth-coming, would probably come from a passer-by who saw somebody slipping through the door of the Admiral Byng. The street was badly lighted but lucky chances were the very stuff of police work. "Now," he said a trifle wryly, "we come to Sergeant Humphrey's contribution. So far as it goes, it comes to the fact that Miss Melusina Drago has nothing to contribute, and there is not any weapon at our command to force her to try. The law does not prohibit a woman from pretending to be a wife: one suspects we should have a large proportion of our daughters in the lock-up if that were so. I did get on to our theatrical contact and her real name is Mabel Drake, born thirty-five years ago to a couple who ran a boarding house at Blackpool, a big prosper-ous one according to the local police. In her teens she helped her parents run it, but when they retired she came to London and went to drama school. They were a large family and her share—which was apparently given her to pursue her studies—was nothing spectacular. She is competent, TV work, minor film and stage engagements, at one time had a night-club act and does a certain amount of modelling, but it is a precarious living if you are not very good. She fits into a certain world composed of similar people and when not working usually manages to dine out or go to a party. No known men permanently in her life, shares a flat at six guineas a week each with four other ladies in Highgate.

"I do not know whether we could get her positively identified from the pub side of it. Oh, people in pubs, a few drinks in, are very positive, but get them cold sober next day and they hum and haw. What impresses me is that she presumably knew catering. Most of the women in her circle can barely use grease and a frying-pan." The Commander shuddered. "To run the catering side of a large public house requires expertise which rather pinpoints her and she must know a lot about the late Alwyn. Sergeant Humphrey, take this address and go to see her. She is not working, apart from modelling assignments. I suggest that you assume the role of an aspiring young man who is going to get it in the neck if he does not come up with results. She is some years older than you, so let her be a mother to you."

"Yes, sir," said Humphrey, reflecting what a cynical old beast the Commander was.

"Has she got a large bosom?"

Flustered, Humphrey said, "I don't, I mean I did not notice it, sir."

"Whatever its size, weep on it." With that the Commander went on to Item 2 of the Agenda, an elderly Pakistani who had been chased by skinheads until he had had a heart attack.

The woman whom Sergeant Reed went to see was known among her intimates as the Duchess, and unless you knew that she liked Bacardi rum and dirty stories you might take her for one, although perhaps even then you might, depending on your experience of duchesses.

The number of people who are prepared to believe that somebody in the United States, recently deceased, has left thirty thousand dollars (the sum is traditional) to people of the same name in the United Kingdom providing they are of strictly honest character hardly varies from decade to decade, just as in the United States a certain number of persons per year are prepared to pay a deposit on Brooklyn Bridge or its equivalent.

Slightly harassed, immeasurably genteel, her hats a wee bit eccentric (she was in her prime in 1928), the Duchess usually staged a pratfall, the mark gallantly hauling her to her feet : or, apparently exhausted, she would sit herself on the next deck chair or park seat. In whichever case the Duchess would bemoan the fact that some rough American —'one is afraid definitely uncouth'—whom she had met at Lady Somebody's hunting box five years ago had unfeelingly left her as executor. There came the discovery that the mark bore the very name of the clan to whom the Duchess was giving the money. "How positively wonderful!" the Duchess would remark. There transpired to be just one snag, the Uncouth American having stipulated that to show good will the recipient would have, as a formality, to deposit some cash with the Duchess overnight.

On an average she made one coup per month, averaging three hundred pounds, without liability to income tax, in the days when, Reed thought nostalgically, a quid was a quid and whisky twelve and six a bottle. Over the years she had been convicted three times, spending in all four years 'inside'.

Old now and retired, she had the old-age pension plus private resources—she had put her money in gold shares on general principles, reasoning that the Stock Market was merely a refinement on her own trade. Now, in her cosy flat, she was occasionally visited by her sons and grandchildren— though she had been too cautious ever to marry. To her satisfaction the sons were trade-union officials, to the Duchess's mind an occupation combining the best of both worlds.

She had a cast-iron stomach and was consuming a bowl

54

of pâté and a loaf of new bread in her kitchen when Reed arrived without notice.

"Come in, my old dear," she purred, leading the way to the large kitchen and without any ado fetching out the bottle of rum and some Cokes.

"And what are you after, naughty boy?" she asked, her big, innocent cow's eyes flickering over him.

"How's business?"

"Fair," she said, "fair. It provides a bit of extra income."

In fact the Duchess ran a little employment agency, catering for old female lags who had retired. If you wanted a nice old lady to go round pawnbrokers flogging a gold watch belonging to their late husband (son sometimes worked better, softening the heart of the unwary pawnbroker) the Duchess would provide one. One of her ladies had disposed of sixty stolen watches and an antique pistol in one morning.

Similarly, if the boys wanted to rig a fake auction in the country, they would hire an empty house, fill it with fakes and apply to the Duchess for an apple-faced old widow lady, relict of a prominent something or other, according to how the mood took her, to act as a front and lull the buyers into a sense of security. Dubious antique shops had 'manageresses' from the Duchess's stable, similarly the shady kind of accommodation address.

Apart from the fact that even hard-hearted policemen felt reluctant to put ladies of seventy-odd (seventy was the Duchess's rule, as having reached the age of discretion) in gaol, the villains themselves, as part of the contract, specifically absolved the lady if they were caught. She had no idea what it was all about. It was as well to abide by the agreement, because the Duchess and her ladies had over the years acquired a large variety of acquaintances, and after two defaulters had had boiling water poured over their heads in prison laundries there had been no trouble.

The Duchess occasionally handed Reed useful information in return for a *quid pro quo*. Occasionally she wanted information as to persons and events and generally the plump policeman saw his way clear to oblige over a glass of rum. There was a ritual about it. Not until a piece of pâté had been eaten and the *Cuba libras* remade did Reed say: "There was a delivery made around three months ago," and tell her the details.

"Much trouble?" enquired the Duchess.

"None for the lady as far as I can see."

"Let me see," said the Duchess, who at seventy-eight still carried her account books in her head. Presently she said. "I got a telephone call. I did not recognise the caller. That sometimes happens. It was a man, with a rough voice, though it's easy to fake that. Could I find somebody to go to the address at nine in the morning and wait until noon? I'd get fifteen nicker and a key through the post. It was to accept delivery of a tin trunk. A man named Mr. Bull would call before noon and take it away. There would be another fiver as final payment. The apartment would be closed and both of them would make off.

"I said O.K. It meant four pounds for me and little fish are sweet. So I thought of Kath with the Bloomers. Old Kath hasn't been having it so good, what with a couple of worthless sons who haven't the sense to keep on the outside. The wives aren't much cop, so Kath runs the household and she's eighty-one if a day. I can remember her in her heyday, robbing the department stores blind. She could fade into the landscape and knew all the tricks of disguise, though she always had to wear specs. It was said she could stow twice as much in her grafting bloomers as any other operator. Sometimes she boasts that during a sale at Gamages she stowed away eight commercial-type meat grinders, which I don't believe on account of the rough edges and the clinking. But she was a demon and could do the *mechera* lay when skirts were worn long."

Reed was suitably impressed. The *mecheras* had been gone since before he joined the Force. Often gypsy, they could drop articles on the floor and sheerly by ankles and knees hook them on to sharp staples attached to a petticoat, their hands remaining in full sight to distract attention.

"Closed-circuit TV put an end to her, dear, the beaks getting nasty towards her in spite of her age. You'd think *they* would show a bit of respect for our grey hairs." The Duchess primped her own immaculately dressed and dyed locks for a moment.

"Who called for the trunk?" asked Reed.

"No need for you to bother old Kathie, she having enough troubles of her own. It was a woman, my dear. She said 'Bull's in bed with his back. I'm Mrs. Bull and here is your fiver.' In the afternoon Kathie came to see me for the rest of her money. Quite put out, she was, bless her. I questioned her. Mrs. Bull was a powerful blonde, about five feet eight or nine, with muscles on her. It was a nippy morning and she wore a longish mac, but Kathie knows how to use what eyesight she's got. Blonde means nothing nowadays, what with the wigs and the improved dyes. She thought the dame was a well-preserved fifty-five who had the money for expensive make-up.

"Kathie pointed to the trunk and said, 'What about the carryin'?' not wishing at her age to get mixed up with such things. 'Leave it to me,' said Mrs. Bull, hefting it like a man. 'You get along, I'll follow.' So Kath got."

"Did this Mrs. Bull, who I suspect was missing on one syllable, possess transport?"

"Kathie didn't hang around. You know my instructions —'Don't learn anything you haven't *got* to know'."

Reed courteously poured out the next round of rum and Coke. They meditated companionably. Then Reed said: "Do you get this class of job very often, Duchess?"

"More often than you might think, Reed. People want an anonymous intermediary who won't cross them, so they come to me. My old girls are straight and know all the tricks. If you give 'em a small packet, which is what it generally is, or more rarely a five-pound parcel, nobody is going to con it off them. And violence, well my dear if anybody was to hit one of my girls on the head when they were working for me they'd wish they had never been born. And their families as well." She said it in a quiet genteel voice. But for the fumes of rum she could have been a life peer discussing how to Improve the Working Class, more so really because of her impeccable accent.

"Any theories?"

"It wasn't jewels or dope," said the Duchess, "not in that size. Kathie took a pull at the trunk, with her gloves still on of course, and said it wasn't heavy enough for gold, but had that dead weight which paper has."

"When can I return the favour?" asked Reed, getting up.

"Perhaps next week," said the Duchess. ·

Reed went to see the estate agent who handled the flats, a sly little man who first brightened when he assessed the value of the Sergeant's suit, but relapsed when he read the professional card and heard his errand.

"We've done a mighty job on that block, Sergeant, though I blow my own trumpet, a mighty job. A very difficult assignment as I told the owner, but then I specialise in difficult ones. I'll give you a few of my cards: one never knows when a really go-ahead firm will be needed.

"Let me see, we got the letting contract five months ago. They are pulling the building down exactly eleven months from now. The old agreements lapsed, and they wanted new ones for a year only, squeezing the last pips from the old orange, so to say. That is difficult, because they were unfurnished and nobody likes to furnish a place on one year's tenancy, stands to reason. If I could have advertised five years I'd have rented them over twenty-four hours. As it was we sweated. Dozens of people coming in, looking and deciding 'not'."

"What was the procedure?"

"Having only a limited number of staff, it was more than flesh and blood could bear to escort them personally around the desirable premises, as we coined the phrase for the advertising. Dozens, scores of applicants called in, all eager until we revealed the terms of the tenancy. But most of them decided they would have a look anyway, so I had twenty keys cut, gave one to each applicant and told them to return it when they had finished. And all were returned by the three or four hundred eager applicants. When the happy moment of letting occurred I destroyed them and had the locks changed."

"Did you keep a record of the names?"

"Yes," said the agent, "but once it was let I destroyed it. A clean desk," he glanced at the overflowing ashtray, "is my motto."

Reed thanked him.

Sergeant Humphrey, use of an official car refused, journeyed to Highgate by public transport, deserted at that hour so that the dirt showed up in the bleak, cold light. Presumably Melusina Drago had boy friends with cars or used taxis a lot, because the flat, one of three, was in a remote and very repellent square. Hers was the top one. There were five name cards beside the door bell and a strong smell of deodorant spray.

"Oh!" Miss Drago was far less than cordial.

"An official visitation one is afraid, miss," said Humphrey, following the book. "I could ask you to come to the nearest station unless you think it would be more convenient inside."

Humphrey had no power whatsoever to force Miss Drago to go to any police station, but he omitted to say so.

"Oh, come in!" Her voice sounded weary, though she did not look so. Well groomed in her lace slacks and see-through blouse, she led him into the big living-room. It was clean, but not neat. It must call for a great deal of discipline for so many people to live in what was to say the least constrained circumstances, thought the Sergeant.

It wasn't too bad, reflected Humphrey with the smugness of one who lived with his mother, a virulently house-proud woman. The food was probably fry-ups or nasty little continental muck-ups—the Sergeant dearly loved his ma's steak-and-kidney pudding and had never been able to fathom why his father had taken off one morning with a girl who could neither sew, clean nor cook—he had his mother's reiterated word for it.

"Sit down," said Melusina, glancing at the telephone. From his girl friend's friends the Sergeant was familiar with that reflexive look, common to ladies who relied upon doing most of their eating out.

"We know about the Blackpool boarding house," said Humphrey, "which qualified you to undertake catering for a pub very competently. Positive identification could be such a bore. Suppose you just help us by a little voluntary statement."

"It was quite long ago," she said slowly, "it's only that it was an unpleasant episode, one of the things that your mind rejects. I'd been gambling, so easy to do, such nice men, until one day I owed fourteen hundred pounds. Suddenly they were not very nice men at all. It was quite a shock. The best deal they offered me was to work for them entertaining tourists. A shill is the technical term. Be very nice to the sucker and keep him at the tables, particularly if he has been winning. They don't like winners at all.

"Trouble is," her eyes were cold, "*I* don't like men much. It would have been a God-damn purgatory. Somebody offered me a way out." She reached forward and opened a cigarette box, lighting one before Humphrey could get to his feet. It was *negro* tobacco, the coarse, pungent Spanish or South American type. She was a nervous smoker and Humphrey sat there and let her puff away.

"Who was somebody?" he said at last.

"Oh God! Once you *start* talking! Hell, it was Reg Gaukroger. I had told June a bit about it. She said she would get Gaukroger to lend me the fourteen hundred. I was cold on the offer. If you borrow you make bad friends"—a flash of honest north-country peeped through the trained accent—

"and to be frank the Gaukrogers have been useful friends over the years. Then Gaukroger said he knew a man named Harry Alwyn who had an unusual proposition. I went round to the flat they had at that time and Alwyn was there. He wanted a woman to pose as his wife and help him run a pub."

"Why?"

"I have no idea," she lied.

He let it go, and asked, "You lived at the Admiral Byng?"

"No, I had a room elsewhere. I used to leave around eleven thirty and get in around eleven next day. Mostly I bossed the catering. It was not too hard: there was a good chef and we managed. Sometimes I worked in the bar. Alwyn was rather keen that I showed myself."

"Because he was passing you off as his wife to the licensing police?"

"That was his business. The deal was for a year. He would pay off the gambling debt and give me a barmaid's wages as a member of the staff. I left a year to the day."

"Who were the gamblers you owed the money to?"

"Look, Sergeant, you know as well as I do that you do not talk about men like that. I prefer to preserve my face such as it is."

"What was Alwyn like?"

"He was a smooth operator, if you know what I mean. That sort are difficult to weigh up." She mimicked in Cockney, "A puffick gentleman I'm sure, dear. And for all I know he was."

"He received stolen goods," said Humphrey.

"That was why he was murdered?"

"As good a supposition as any other."

"And therefore as good a reason why I should not talk."

"You have some duty as a citizen," said Humphrey, quoting the book. "And while it sounds quite pompous none of us would perhaps be alive if we totally ignored the obligation."

"You are a policeman," said Melusina Drago, quite kindly, "and the prying little men you have will have told you the kind of life I lead. Mind you, I *like* it. I could not honestly say I would have chosen another. I know I'm a good third-rate actress but nothing else would give me any pleasure. The week-ends at Cannes do not, but the minutes I spend on stage make up for it. Yet I am vulnerable : women in my position are."

"Look, Miss Drago, I got my bottom kicked because of last night. If I go back to the gentry and report it is still no go I shan't be able to get married as there will be no promotion. My boss asked if you had big knockers."

"What!" Melusina glanced down.

"Whatever size, he suggested I weep on them," said Humphrey. "So now you know it all."

Melusina laughed. "Let's throw the weeping-on thing out of the window. Can you promise me not to quote? I assure you I have no knowledge of Alwyn's murder."

"I just want background, which in any case is seldom admissible as evidence. What the soldier said, etcetera."

"I thought that Alwyn used to get a few wide boys in to see him," she said. "It was, probably is, oh, so very respectable City gents in the pricier parts of the pub, and chars and doorkeepers swigging a refreshing pint in the public. Harry was not a bad host. He was good at names and could ask 'How's the old trouble?' as convincingly as publicans do. But a few of the customers did not fit in. They usually drank in a little corner in the saloon where they could not be overheard talking to Alwyn. In the mornings shortly after opening usually. The only other customers were generally a few salesmen and the local bookmaker girding himself for the fray with a double whisky."

"Recognise any of them?"

"I honestly did not. I don't associate with crooks because they mean bad trouble. Yet I've mixed around : friends have pointed some very ropy kind of people out to me. If you sit at a sidewalk café by the Mediterranean with a knowledgeable gossip you see some very funny people. I once saw a professional killer who has an international practice. A rubicund little man. Then again, working as an actress you are taught to type people, and if you watch some of the top-liners they can underline small points of character. Some of the men who came to see Alwyn were shady, if not sooty."

"Did anything change hands?"

"Good God, no. I thought I told you that Harry was smooth and shrewd. The men who came in were not Bill Sykes and he was no Fagin."

"You were dealing with professionals."

"True."

"I appreciate, Miss Drago, that stage training might enable you to recognise types, but the professional crook is an adept at misdirection." Humphrey smiled wryly. "I would not be quoted on this, but things have been stolen under our very noses, sometimes purely as a dare."

"I would say that if anything changed hands, a packet or small parcel, it must have been very small indeed. He might have arranged the transactions there, but the exchange took place elsewhere."

"You knew the staff well?"

"Nobody lasts eight years these days in anything. There was a head barman named Pollick who knew his job through and through."

"He's still there."

"I never went back after the day I left. Alwyn gave me a fifty-pound bonus on that condition. It meant nothing to me."

"Miss Drago, was Alwyn the kind of man to be celibate?"

She laughed again. "I do not imagine so. But you must let me think about this one, but not for too long as I have a modelling engagement."

"I don't want to harp on it," said Melusina after a couple of minutes, "but the Gaukrogers are very useful to me. Superb food at least once a week, a house at Ascot during the racing, a cottage in the country near Port Isaac in Corn-wall which I can use. So, please, oh, please do not put me in."

"I will not," said Humphrey. The smell of women about the place was making him drowsy and bed inclined.

"June Gaukroger is younger than me. At one time she did the usual modelling course they all take nowadays: I was doing instructing in voice production if they wanted an extra subject. We became friendly. I suppose she was nineteen, though she was already married to Reg Gaukroger. Harry Alwyn was her lover. I never met him until I got into this trouble, but she told me about him."

Humphrey felt rather young. "It seems a bit young for a married woman to have . . . isn't the term paramour?"

"It does sound saucy put that way, French and all that jazz. Reg and June are a bit peculiar in that it was simply a marriage of convenience."

"That's always a difficult term."

"They went their own way. Gaukroger is vulgar, but he knows money. June, or rather her mother, has a great deal of money. They suit each other. Reg is a wheeler-dealer who can sell anything. He picked up a hundred thousand frying-pans once, all rusty round the edges, and sold them next day for a little profit on each. He is not quite *true*, a bit larger than life, but that kind of man always is."

"How long did it last?"

"I think it lasted to the end. She was very cut up last night. That is why she hit the bottle—she is nothing like a lushington normally. Reg was upset on her behalf. He is not an unkind man. It's his sense of inferiority that forces him to have all these parties."

Why the hell did Freud always have to barge in to police work, wondered Humphrey and not for the first time. He thought a gin might dispel his drowsiness, but there was not a bottle in sight. Rarely a drinker—his mother attributed his father's sins to addiction and the keeping of a bottle inside the steriliser at his dental office—Humphrey consciously forbore to ask. He was not going to get like Reed.

"I suppose it is not possible that Mr. Gaukroger is a crook?"

She laughed. "With the money he turns over, and June's own fortune, I can't see why he should be."

"Tell me, did Mrs. Gaukroger and Alwyn have a little hide-away pad?"

"I dare say it was done in a ladylike and gentlemanly way," said Miss Drago primly.

"Thank you, miss," said Humphrey and went out into the fresh air.

'Crying' Jarvis had tea, laced on the lady's part with a teeny potation of Dutch gin which somebody had assured her was a specific for her kidneys, which like most of her other organs caused trouble. Her name was Belcher and she was not inappropriately styled. A lot of money had gone into the apartment, noted Jarvis. He had, after some cogitation, settled on the liver as a subject of conversation, attributing its frailties to increased air traffic into London.

"Charming people, the Gaukrogers," remarked the Sergeant through a Bath bun. "Though at the rate they were drinking I shouldn't be surprised if they don't get a bit of trouble. Nothing like Scotch to touch up the old liver."

"My father, God rest him, had spots before the eyes for the last thirty-five years and when they turned green the surgeon said there was nothing human to be done. He'd got up to three bottles." Mrs. Belcher filled her teacup.

"Hard drinkers, eh?" sighed Jarvis.

"I wouldn't say that," observed the good lady, helping herself to another small medicinal potation. "Reg Gaukroger often has a drink in his hand which never goes near his mouth, and June does not drink much but dry Martini, which my father said was a baby drink for wops and people like that. They were upset, my dear, and like other people they tend to fly to the bottle when taken aback."

"A bereavement?" intoned Jarvis, sepulchrally.

"Something very sad," responded Mrs. Belcher with

65

gloomy relish, "an old and intimate family friend was murdered. A Mr. Alwyn."

"Ah," said Jarvis, "I read about that. A publican, but don't think I'm narrow minded, Mrs. Belcher, because there's room for all sorts in the world as the Good Book says. Take a little drop more of your medicine, ma'am. The only reason I do not is because of What the Doctor Told Me about my condition, but it varies from person to person as stands to reason. I suppose you knew Mr. Alwyn?"

"Once or twice I met him. Mrs. Stoney used to have him for lunch sometimes."

Mrs. Stoney. It struck a chord. There was a line of coloured photographic prints on the mantelpiece which he had not noticed before. Jarvis had an almost perfect memory for faces, and of the ten prints two were known to him. Of course, there was the late Bob Belcher, with his neat moustache and vaguely ecclesiastical appearance, who had passed away during the effort of passing eighteen years in one of Her Britannic Majesty's establishments for running an entirely bogus insurance company. His relict, realised the Sergeant, must be very warm indeed financially.

And Mrs. Stoney was there, her large blond smiling face leering out of the print. Why had he not recognised her at the party? Probably, thought Jarvis, because he had not expected to meet her at the Gaukrogers. There had been a Mr. Stoney, but he had considered it desirable to 'go through' to West Australia, where he had served a few prison sentences for armed robbery. He remained there because he was safe from the wrath of his wife who had resented his repeated infidelities. She had been the only child of London's biggest illegal bookmaker who had received stolen diamonds as a very profitable sideline. He had died, in an odour of sanctity, quite a few years ago. In her youth Mrs. Stoney had been her dad's right hand and an adept at taking hot jewellery over to Holland. Jarvis had not heard of her for years.

"Who is Mrs. Stoney?" he asked. "I can only remember her vaguely."

"You were probably only told that she was June Gaukroger's mum," said Mrs. Belcher comfortably.

Fifteen years older than the photograph, thought Jarvis, and two stone heavier. She had fairly gobbled at the canapés, but he remembered that her china-blue eyes had missed nothing, particularly nothing that Reg Gaukroger did.

"Her father was an old friend of my husband," said Mrs. Belcher, "before he developed Business Misfortunes and passed away in an Institution, so we have something in common."

Jarvis helped himself to another Bath bun. "Does Mrs. Stoney help in Mr. Gaukroger's business?" he asked. "From something she said, I thought that she might."

"Mrs. Stoney has Capital," pontificated Mrs. Belcher, "and she finances Reg." Abruptly losing interest in the subject she switched to a Liver, presenting curious problems, which belonged to an old friend.

CHAPTER THREE

A T S E V E N O ' C L O C K the Commander, after having
digested the reports, reluctantly repaired to the Admiral
Byng. It was his duty to inspect the scene of the crime,
though in these days when forensic photography was a science
he could not think why, except that the Home Secretary
expected it. Knowing the proclivity of the British public to
ogle and leer at places where violent death has taken place,
an activity, the Commander thought, which even took pre-
cedence over beating children and abandoning puppies on
main roads, he was not surprised to find the pub bursting
at the seams. Mr. Will Pudding, representing the omniscient
Brewery, had engaged six temporary staff and presided like
a slightly drunken deity in the little office behind the saloon
bar. The air was thick with tobacco smoke and talk.

Inevitably there was competition to drink at the exact spot
where the late Harry Alwyn had got his skull staved in, a
kind of miniature football scrum, in front of which Joe
Pollick, sweat streaming down his knotted face, and two
assistants shoved over drinks and made change, the coins
moist with beer. The steam radiators were on, but the heat
was mainly from a multitude of bodies.

From his great height, which with his patrician appearance
and background had assured him of a settled position among
the Establishment, the Commander saw the features of Sergeant Reed, beer froth on the bridge of his nose. Beside him
was Sergeant—what was the fellow's name? ah yes,
Humphrey—drinking from a smaller glass. Sounded like a
sex maniac, thought the Commander. Have to watch him
like a hawk. Breaking beds! Chilblains! A likely story. The
Commander remembered an unfortunate personal experience
in an Elizabethan bed wherein he had got mixed up with

the canopy, requiring the services of a knowing butler to extricate him and the lady. But it was one thing at country house parties organised for people of decent family and quite another for prolly sergeants. Somebody jolted him. The Commander looked down with distaste, but it was Sergeant Jarvis, virtuously displaying a glass of soft drink. For a moment the Commander felt a glow of approbation, but then soured at the memory of Jarvis's long history of financial fiddling which had caused Superintendent Quant to mark his personal file 'not fit for further promotion'.

"Have you noticed the faces, sir?" asked Jarvis out of the corner of his mouth, a trick common to crooks and policemen. The Commander, coming into the brilliantly lighted bar—Alwyn must have had a thing about lighting—from the dark street had barely had time to focus. Now he looked around, my word, there were some familiar faces around from the upper, almost respectable echelon of the underworld. In the corner was Dr. Dee, bald and seventy, with his attractive raven-headed wife, twenty years younger and according to some people the brains of the combination.

In fact at seven o'clock that morning Dr. Dee, a man of dubious origin who claimed a Rumanian degree in philology, had hit his wife across the chops while sitting up in bed drinking tea from the automated electric dispenser. The good doctor, a powerful though quite hairless man, was in the habit of doing this when agitated. He thought in Croat, but had long disciplined himself into talking English.

"Shut up, you bitch," he had said. "Your croaking won't make it better."

"The money, Doctor," his wife had said. "Our retirement money."

Dee propelled her out of bed by a violent flexing of his knees. With gloomy satisfaction he heard the electric blanket tear and, reaching out, poured the hot tea down her nightgown.

"The money would be in the public house," he said, "probably buried in the little backyard."

Seated on the carpet, Mrs. Dee expostulated, "Too noisy. In a cask perhaps. Knock the top off a cask, put the notes in, and replace it."

She was useful, ruminated Dee, otherwise he would have got rid of her long ago when she started getting creaky.

"Pick your teeth up," he said. "God knows they are enough trouble already. We should have lunch at the pub."

"Not lunch," she said, getting to her feet. "They are all City men and know each other." She forbore to mention that the hideous, hairless doctor stood out like a sore thumb, a fact which had often caused him to be deported back to England. "But at night there will be sight-seers and we can be like mice among them."

"We'll have to employ somebody," said Dr. Dee. "We must look at the locks. You are probably right, it must be in the cellar."

Georgie Thigh and his woman had spotted the Commander's entry.

"Christ! The top brass," he said. "Why the hell did the stoopid bastard get his skull stove in? You tell me."

"I don't suppose he wanted his brains out." Thelma was a saucy little woman who read books and Georgie was a bit afraid of her.

"I hope he didn't keep no records," said Georgie, who spoke perfect French but bad English.

"Be your age! Why the hell should he keep records here?"

"He'd have to keep them *somewhere*," Georgie muttered. "There are a lot of plices in a pub. This is a right old gaff, goes back years, and it would have these old cellars. Bloody great plices they were: I bin down one or two; old casks, things like that. Easy to stuff a notebook in."

"The demons'd think of that," said Thelma, "and search the place to pieces."

"They aren't after that side," said Georgie. "They are after a killer. I'll have to get in and tike a look-see at that cellar. I dunno about that effing great lock and the windows are barred. I better get young Alfred to work on the door. It's quiet round here around three in the mornin'. The delivery trucks don't start until five."

"Is it a risk you should take, darl?"

"Next time," said Georgie quietly, "it's an indeterminate sentence, luv. Umpteen effing years until I ain't got teeth, let alone . . ."

"Let's bolt for it. We got fourteen thousand pounds."

"They pick you up," said Georgie, gloomily, "even in Australia where the coppers are half blind all the time."

"It'll have to be you and Alfred then," said Thelma, "and I'll drive the car. Get false plates on it."

"Might take a couple of days," said Georgie, "and thirty quid."

"Worth it," opined his *de facto*.

They always said a man could *straighten* Sergeant Reed, the immense person known simply as Fat, sex unknown, was thinking as he toyed with a brandy and Benedictine. Unfortunately the only person he knew who had tried it had mysteriously fallen down a flight of stone stairs and knocked his teeth out. But there were too many coppers around. His eyes, winking though folds of scabby flesh, were never still. Behind him his two minders stirred uneasily, recognising the boss's mood which so often meant trouble. Both eased the cut-throat razor under the left coat lapel in spring clips.

He was wondering if Harry Alwyn had left an organisation behind him. Fat had recently acquired a collection of sovereigns, priceless on the Indian market. Alwyn used to handle the foreign trade so well that Fat had come to rely upon him, something he rarely did. It had dawned upon him that where there was death there were pickings: he had a childhood memory of two aunts quarrelling bitterly over his mother's coat after her demise, an altercation which Fat, aged seven, had solved by taking the ancient garment through the window and flogging it to the local pawnbroker for two and ninepence. Fat wondered if he should buy the pub. A licence was impossible for him, but a company could be formed, with a manager. The knobbly man behind the bar, Pollick was his name Fat remembered, might make a willing stooge. Nothing fancy, just smooth, as Harry Alwyn had run it. With the Common Market in sight Fat, through interpreters, had had conversations with the French and Belgian boys and the prospect of international co-operation had never looked better than under the beneficent European umbrella. Armaments, whore houses, diamonds and smuggled Australian beef had been discussed : it would be a time of lush pastures. Fat licked his lips.

"I think we should give them back," Valerie was saying, in the rather neighing voice that had cost her father plenty to finance. She was born to strife, so it appeared to her parents, never a university scrimmage being complete without her being dragged into the police van, screaming and hanging on to a banner bearing a slogan whose meaning passed out of her baldish head three months later.

Timothy, her boy friend, who seemed to his parents destined to study economics for the rest of his natural life without coming to much conclusion, was in contrast very hairy and short in stature. He was wrinkling his lips and thinking of ethical values.

It had been an odd time to go to Lisbon, just after Christmas, but Timothy had been subsidised for a crash course in Portuguese. He had taken Valerie on an even-steven financial basis to Lisbon. In one of the rather fabulous little restaurants they had been approached by a charming, svelte young man. Could they, for fifty pounds, take a tiny package to London? A rare medicine needed by his old auntie, the young man had said with a leer. The teachings of the London

72

School of Economics had made Timothy accept with alacrity. They had of course opened the packet back at the hotel. There were ten rubies, unset, but which to their untutored eyes looked very large. Cautiously, Timothy had devised a scheme by which Valerie sewed them—not that she was much good at sewing—into her sparse underwear. Instructions had been to go this evening to the Admiral Byng and give their names to the proprietor. Somebody would take delivery of the packet, now restored, its contents removed from Valerie's midriff to her handbag.

('If they bloody well catch us,' Timothy was thinking, 'I'll deny any knowledge. Six months inside would serve the bitch right.' Valerie could be very trying at times.)

"To who?" he said aloud. "The man's dead, curse him."

"There are the people behind the bar."

Valerie was always talking about destroying decadent society and substituting something else which she was uncertain about, thought Timothy who privately considered it was a bloody good society to leech upon. But intellectually she was a nit who could not destroy anything, capable of brandishing these rubies around while asking incriminating questions. She was the type of moron who could not even kidnap a West German ambassador, which God knew seemed a piece of cake. Thriftily he finished his glass of stout and shoving two old ladies mercilessly aside plonked the glass on the counter.

"I'm off," he said shortly and pushed his way through the throng.

"Timothy," neighed Valerie as his nuggety behind disappeared. The fact that she was holding a largely untasted Campari and soda, and that it was impossible for her to reach over to the counter, immobilised her. As she turned she bumped into the belly of a medium-sized, cherubic man who smelt strongly of ale. "Perhaps I could help you, miss," he suggested.

Valerie goggled at him.

"C.I.D.," he said, "name of Reed."

Valerie, still clutching her drink, scuttled sideways and with rare presence of mind stooped and placed the glass on the floor, where a foot immediately overturned it. Lowering her head in the manner learned from many demos she butted her way through the crowd, her monstrous girth creating a kind of wake. Reed looked on, slightly amused, but puzzled.

Big Bertie, who was in fact all of five feet two inches, was drinking with his long-standing friend Johnny, who towered above everybody else in the bar except the Commander.

"He was getting out, anyway," said Bertie philosophically, "or so he told me. He wanted to get a bit of sun on his back every day."

"He couldn't get out," said Johnny, a thinker, "because you can't. Once you're in, you are bloody well in."

"Here we are," said Big Bertie dismally, "with four thousand quid's worth of stuff to flog outside the country, and he dies on us."

"There'll be another," said Johnny.

"You could trust Harry Alwyn," said Bertie, "which you can't with most of the effers. See over there, that old bastard Dee! Alwyn would have paid without argy-bargy. Dee would offer twenty per cent."

"I'll cut his throat one of these days if I can do it safely," said Johnny quite calmly. "However he's an old bloke and can't go on for ever. Have you thought that Harry must have had quite a bit of loot stashed away?"

"Here?"

"Don't see why not."

"That front door is a hard one," said Bertie.

"Doors are made to go through," said Johnny, "and we've got the gear."

"Lot of police around," muttered Bertie.

"Only today and tomorrow. They can't learn anything here. Harry wasn't the kind of man to spread info around. If he's got anything it would be in the cellar, safe as houses.

We might take a look. No real risk." He laughed. "We could get the lawyer to plead guilty to being on licensed premises after hours and it would probably stick. Fifty quid or one month under the lock."

"You are a one," camped Bertie.

"As prime a collection of burglars and fences as one has seen in a confined space," muttered the Commander to Sergeant Jarvis.

"Pity we can't get a mandatory gaol sentence for consorting together like they have in Australia. I suppose we could pull them on suspicion."

"Nothing we could justify," growled the Commander, "there would be questions asked in the House by all the old women there."

"I wonder what they are here for," said Jarvis. "Revisiting the scene of the crime? But all of them couldn't have killed him!"

"There must be a cellar here," said the Commander, "I don't suppose they looked at it."

"A cellar, sir?"

"If you run a pub it's the ideal place to conceal anything. From memory the entrance in these old places was a trapdoor in the floor of the public bar. Let's go and see."

The Commander led the way. It was less crowded by a long chalk than the saloon. There was set into the floor a large trapdoor with counterset rings at each corner.

"Can't do it until the crowd is gone," muttered the Commander, looking at his watch. "I have an appointment in Whitehall. You fellows hang on and see to it."

Probably looking forward to a genial boozy evening at one of his clubs, reflected Sergeant Jarvis gloomily as he sought out Reed and Humphrey. By some alchemy Reed had procured a secluded little corner of the bar and was arguing with Mr. Pudding, representing the Brewery, over the merits and defects of placing a little raspberry juice in a glass of lager.

"Inhuman, the Brewery would say," opined Mr. Pudding. "Inhuman and against all Nature. Muck about with beer, sir, and it will muck about with you and that includes mulling it or adding gin."

Reed introduced Jarvis who incurred a beady look when he ordered a glass of grapefruit. "It's a touch of the old ulcers," he hastened to explain.

"Whatever happened to that missing bottle of Chartreuse?" The thought hit Reed sharply.

"We never found it," said Mr. Pudding. "Neither hide nor hair of it."

"Did you see the last Forensic?" asked Humphrey.

"No," said Reed.

"They think it was a round bottle, holding about a pint. He was hunched over the bar with somebody standing beside him. They picked up the bottle and that was that. Death instantaneous."

"Have a round on the Brewery, gennelmen." Mr. Pudding had gone a little green. "What a way to treat good liquor, I'm sure."

"Probably carried it away with him—or her—for a libation later," quipped Reed. "And, Mr. Pudding, what do you know about the cellarage?"

"Don't tell me the Monster is down there, lurking. What my Chairman would say I shudder to think."

"Monsters don't hang around in cellars," said Reed looking reflectively at the line of people along the bar. "He's more likely to be nibbling a beer up here. But do you know what is down the cellar, like equipment?"

"It hasn't been used these fifteen years. I remember it. A hairy old place twenty foot deep and very large. This place used to be a beer and gin house when Vickie, God bless her, was on the throne. By God, you could get drunk for twopence and it was the makin' of the Brewery. The great, grey horses, sirs, and the men on them like horses themselves. A

76

free eight-gallon cask each got once a week from the Brewery and that represented just a little wet before breakfast. Steak and chops is what they ate, fried on a shovel. They used to manhandle the cases and casks down the stairs. The beer had to be 'fined' by the Publican himself and there was a rare art in it."

"I suppose you can get down into the ruddy place?" asked Jarvis irritably, for there was a poetic twist to Mr. Pudding's beery enunciation—Jarvis supposed the man was Welsh—and the Sergeant loathed poesy.

"Iron stairs flank the ramp," confided the Brewery representative.

"And the contents?" insisted Reed.

"Like the business man that he was, the late Mr. Alwyn kept a list which is in my pocket now."

'It' proved to be a neatly bound, loose-leaf black book.

"The publican's bible," said Pudding. "Here we are—cellarage. 'No longer used. Electric light and water in good order. Fifty old wine cases with bottles, three derelict beer casks. Racks and shelves in fair order.' "

"Half an hour to go and the crowd thinning out, novelty over," said Reed. "With your permission, sir, we'd like a brief look-see after closing."

"The Brewery has pleasure in assenting," Mr. Pudding bowed unsteadily.

" 'Ere, I say, you're the copper I met yesterday." It was Mrs. Crippen, the cleaner, remembered Sergeant Reed, now clad in what appeared to be an outsize boiler suit. "I come in to oblige the Brewery, tonight bein' a thick 'un." She gave the approximation of a curtsy to Mr. Pudding, the outward and visible sign of the Brewery's grace, and he flapped one tremulous old hand in acknowledgment.

"I fahned this on the floor hinside the door." She extended an unexpectedly large, if grimy, hand on which reposed a piece of paper with ten red stones on it.

"Rubies, ain't they?"

"Might be coloured glass."

"Well, if so I'll just keep them."

"Everything must be handed in to the police if found," said Sergeant Humphrey, rushing in.

Mrs. Crippen cackled. "Oh, young man, suppose I 'anded you a . . ." The old lady became unprintable and Humphrey blushed.

"Now, my old dear," said Reed, "if claimed there will be a nice reward to buy you and yours a blow-out at Margate. If unclaimed they will probably be yours and you can buy a pub."

"We'd only drink ourselves to death," she said, but handed over the stones. "Don't forget the name is Mrs. Crippen of Fourteen, Dodge Road."

"Are they real?" asked Humphrey, as Reed spread them on the bar.

The Sergeant, who knew something about stones, peered. "I would think so. They look it."

"How much?" asked Jarvis, avarice in his voice.

"You need a glass and a pair of scales. They are not superfine stones. Say four thousand the lot wholesale, and two thousand fenced. Why, hullo, Big Bertie," Reed's hand shot out and gripped the small burglar by one wrist.

A good man in brawls or troubles, Sergeant Jarvis got his own back against the partition wall and Reed noticed unfriendly eyes along the bar.

But Big Bertie said swiftly, "Only a squiz, guv'nor, as I was walking along to the gents."

The gents was in the other direction, but Reed merely released his grip and nodded, putting the stones in his trouser pocket. Big Bertie walked off.

"Rubies, Johnny," Big Bertie said later as they sat in the back of a cab. "Ten of them, but I couldn't get close enough for a real look-see."

"You took a chance, dear boy," grunted Johnny.

"They knew we were there, Johnny. That fellow Reed has got eyes in his arse."

"Where did they get the stones?"

"Not in the cellar, Johnny, that I'll swear. A fellow like Harry Alwyn could have had stuff stashed all around, in bottles, in the loo cisterns, in his mattress, why there is no end to it."

"Your tongue always runs away with you, dear boy," said Johnny, but with affection, "although we will have to have a look-see at the cellar. I was wondering if old Dr. Dee had him done in. He's got the connections with the Mafia, you know. Suppose one of their 'hit men' came over and finished Harry?"

"But why, Johnny?"

"You should keep your ear to the ground more, dear boy." Johnny was half serious and squeezed the small man's arm until he whimpered. "The bank robbery loot: there's a rumour that it is being flogged around with maybe thirty or forty thou clear to be made. They did *not* take any numbers of the notes as was thought. Suppose it was Harry that was handling it, dear boy. I know Harry was straight, but what a temptation, particularly as you say he wanted to retire. Just suppose he sold the loot twice or something of that nature."

"I've known it happen," whined Big Bertie, rubbing his arm where it hurt. "There was Frankie Lewin who always sold things twice over. Oh dear, the lies he told. They called him the Just Man because he was always just going to deliver the loot but never did."

"He ended in the River did he not, dear boy? Throat nicely cut!"

Big Bertie gave a delicious little shudder. "A friend of mine, oh it was before we *met*, identified him. My dear, he had no face because of the fish."

"Something funny going on there tonight," said Dr. Dee,

not turning his head as he eased the Daimler into motion. "They'd discovered something. That little swine Big Bertie took a look at it. Someone should cut his throat."

"Should we not cut our losses, dear? I feel goose pimples about this one," said Mrs. Dee.

"I paid him five thousand on account," said the Doctor, "against a total payment of twenty thousand. A steal! I might have made thirty thousand in foreign currency, then we could retire to Ischia and live as we have planned to do. Damn it!" The car jolted under his irritation. "The fellow promised the notes to me last week, but he told me that he must have my cheque first and clear it. Oh, that was all right, just business. So I arrange to see him today and the man is dead as a dado"—the good Doctor's English slipped almost imperceptibly when he was irritated. "The notes are mine. I have paid the deposit, no? I have a right to them. I must employ somebody to search that cellar. The front-door lock is a good one, but there are men who could open it. We need three perhaps, who will not doublecross us, not that many would dare."

He was thinking aloud, as was his wont as he grew older. Mrs. Dee already knew all of it. "The Toad and his brothers," she said. "He is too dumb to doublecross."

"But he stands out like a sore Toad," the Doctor giggled at his own joke. "So ugly that people remember him. I was thinking of little Tommy Piper, nobody remembers him, not even his own mother."

"The Toad is better on locks," said Mrs. Dee.

"It shall be Tommy Piper," said the Doctor and raised his left hand from the wheel.

Mrs. Dee kept silent.

"Well," Mr. Pudding was saying to Joe Pollick above the clinking of glasses being washed and the noise from Mrs. Crippen's broom, "it would be about the best evening's work ever done here!" Mr. Pudding divested the tills of their contents and placed them in a Gladstone bag.

"What are you going to do with all that dough?" asked Jarvis, his drink-free palate wincing at the powerful disinfectant that Mrs. Crippen's helper was scattering in her wake.

"Put it in the safe here overnight, bank in the morning. It's a big old safe, but it would take an hour or so to open it." Mr. Pudding had abruptly sobered after a glass of soda water.

"Was there anything in the safe?" asked Humphrey.

Drink did not improve Mr. Pudding's temper at times. He glared at Humphrey. "His keys were given to me by an Inspector of Police and I opened it on behalf of The Brewery. The usual records, sir, and fifty pounds plus ten pounds odd in small change.

"The night's takings," said Pollick. "I cleared the tills and checked it with him. It had been a very poor night because of the weather. You can't anticipate anything in this trade."

"Including being bashed on the head," said Reed between burps, realising he should not have finished off on brandy: it only gave you a thirst and the beer was 'off'.

"Some funny fellows were here tonight," said Jarvis, who still had half a glass of tomato juice. He looked at Pollick. "Did you see a great fat man standing about the middle of the bar, and near him a very tall bod, say six feet four and a bit, accompanied by a short, stubby man?"

"Yes, sir," said Pollick, "but then I've seen them in here before."

"Often?"

"Not regulars, sir, but my impression is that they sometimes dropped in to take a glass with the late Mr. Alwyn."

"There were quite a few others," said Jarvis, "all more or less dangerous crooks."

"It takes all kinds to make a world," said Joe Pollick with barman's philosophy.

"In this case an underworld," grunted Reed.

"The Brewery wouldn't like it," intoned Mr. Pudding.

"You oughta see some of the pubs down Stepney way," said Pollick. "A thousand years of time served drinking in the bigger ones every night and more razors about than at a barbers' conference." The little barman rested a hand on the counter and momentarily dropped his tea-cloth. "There were some grafters that used to come in, and that's a fact, to have a discreet word with the gaffer, but it weren't my business, sir. A lot of publicans have sidelines, some of them honest, some sway-sway and some downright dishonest, but that's up to the police, ennit?"

"Did you ever see anything change hands?" persisted Jarvis.

"I didn't look directly or hard," said Pollick, a dry note in his voice. "This was a decent sort of crib to work in as I told you yesterday. Nevertheless I am pretty sure nothing was passed either way, except maybe money or something very small."

"Let's look at the cellar and get it over," said Humphrey.

"I have news," said Reed. "My cellar-climbing days are at an end. You and Mr. Jarvis look at the cellar while Mr. Pudding and I do our late-night contemplation."

"A small Scotch for yours truly," said Pollick.

Jarvis walked along with Humphrey to the public bar and the two men bent to prise up the hatch, revealing a hole about six feet square. A smell of dampness and an overtone of gas came up to them.

On his knees, Humphrey reached down and clicked on an electric-light switch. The light was poor but adequate. The old iron ramp, with cross pieces to control the descent of the barrels, was at an angle of forty-five degrees. The iron stairs by its side were perpendicular and treacherous.

"You coming?" Humphrey asked.

"Yeah," said Jarvis. "You first, though. The trick would be to hold on to the side of the ramp. Mind you I had a fall once in similar circumstances and it was a lovely eight months on full pay, the doctor being sympathetic. If you do go keep complaining of the dreadful pain. They can't prove to the contrary."

Humphrey lowered himself on to the ladder, clutching the side of the ramp. He at least had no desire for eight invalid months. Jarvis's more ponderous footsteps echoed above him. At the bottom it was truly cold and dank, with the slight smell of decayed cardboard which cellars always seem to have. There was another light switch and the two bulbs were powerful.

"Just another disused cellar," said Jarvis as he arrived and tapped the thick old cement floor. "They used to bury people underneath, but we always got them because the new cement showed, so they've given up doing it that way."

The racks were filled with grimy bottles. Systematically they upended and shook them, with no result.

"Haven't been touched for years," said Humphrey. The old barrels were spider-webbed and greenish looking.

"We'll have to get permission and a cooper to take the heads off," said Jarvis, kicking one. It faintly boomed.

"Nothing here, I think," said Humphrey.

"Better get it searched tomorrow," said the experienced Jarvis. "You have to go over these ruddy places with a tooth comb. I once found fourteen ounces of heroin in a hole which had been plastered over. The technician with me spotted it—they had even stuck an old spider-web over it. Hallo! Good God!"

He had wandered to one side, looking behind the line of barrels.

Humphrey walked forward three paces and looked. Behind the barrels was what might be taken for a bundle of old clothes. A cheap, 'tweed' overcoat surmounted shiny blue trousers, only a face peered out from the bundle, a waxy, very dead face.

Jarvis peered close with professional stoicism. "Funny how your face changes when you die," he observed with mild interest. "But I know him, one Peter Pipchin, a go-between man for years. Any dirty little negotiation and you couldn't

83

do better than Peter. Twice under the lock for extortion. Well, my boy, it's out of bed you and I will be for some hours. Don't forget to put in for the late-night expenses, late-supper money and taxi home."

Like the shrewd old campaigner he is, Sergeant Reed had retired from the pub before the City of London murder squad arrived. He had decided that Mr. Pudding was a man after his own heart, but a brandy had suddenly sent him to sleep and the Sergeant and Joe Pollick had wedged him into a chair.

He breakfasted off beer and salami and was at the Yard on the dot of eight thirty. Chief Superintendent Quant (a little porridge and a cup of weak tea sustaining him) was in no immediate mood to discuss the murder which after all was temporarily the dead pigeon of the City of London Police. He was immersed in the problem of dirty books offending the local library committees and was peering with a puzzled frown at the collected works of various American writers. He rather brightened at Reed's emergence. Most of the younger men merely sniggered when he discussed the problem of Myra Breckinridge. Reed listened patiently.

"With some of them," finished Quant, "ye have to get special permission from the Chief Librarian. He canna refuse you, but he gives ye a stern look up and down." His native Scottish always took command when sex cropped up.

Reed momentarily fingered the grog blossom which flowered on the left side of his snub nose. "They issue cards, you know. I remember reading that in the old days the French police issued yellow identity cards to prostitutes."

"You mean?" said Quant eagerly.

"That librarians be empowered to issue dirty readers with yellow cards to shame them. The librarians could spot them —they are a dirty-minded lot we find. It would put most of the publishers out of business, of course."

"About time some of them were closed down," said Quant

with satisfaction, his ancient fountain pen creaking as he made the note. "The Prime Minister will like this blow for morality, I'm sure."

It was a pity, he thought, that Reed's file was marked 'not for further promotion', for the man was clearly equipped for better things, like cleaning up public morals, which Quant considered in a cesspool state.

The Sergeant felt in his inside pocket and produced the paper with the rubies in it. "Found on the floor of the pub by a cleaner, one Mrs. Crippen."

The Superintendent, who disapproved of 'baubles' on religious grounds—the late Mrs. Quant had never obtained her coveted engagement ring—prodded them with a hairy middle finger. "Real?"

"I put them under a loup at home. They are fair average quality stones, one of them probably better than average. I'll leave them with you, sir."

The Super stolidly entered the transaction in his daily diary.

"Have you any idea who abandoned them?"

"The place was full of crooks and curiosity gogglers, a record evening I should imagine. Anybody could have dropped them on the floor : it's a wonder they were not stamped on. It probably means an amateur, a pro would not have panicked. There is precious little chance of tracing stones of that size, they might have originated anywhere."

Quant said : "The corpse was one Peter Pipchin. Fingerprints confirmed the smart identification by Jarvis. What a night it was apparently! The City Police say death occurred approximately at the same time as Harry Alwyn's." He noticed the Sergeant's rather sceptical look and added, "The temperature in that cellar, a deep one, hardly alters by a degree, so that is the basis of the calculation. We have a lot on Pipchin, who was sixty years old and lived in the Borough. Three convictions, the last for uttering threats in 1939, a serious case out of which he got three years. When he came out he had lost his taste for gaol, they could be

85

tough places in those days and he was in one of the toughest. So he became one of the middlemen, a bit more than a messenger boy, working for five pounds a day. He was discreet and hard to spot in a crowd."

"But how the devil did he get down that cellar?" asked Reed.

"It points to Alwyn," sighed Quant. "The poor little devil was strangled manually and Alwyn had the strength for that. Suppose he lured him down the cellar and finished him off. Safe enough. Nobody ever went down it. He could dispose of the remains at leisure."

"And then somebody murdered Alwyn! He must have known Pipchin, or the person employing him, to let him in. And the second person also must have been known to him. It seems that the Admiral Byng had a very busy night trade."

"I was interested in the head barman," grunted Quant, "but Joe Pollick has had a blameless life, sole support of a widowed family for many years, now living alone in a bed-sitter not too far from his work. Not a womaniser, but drinks a bit after business hours, more fool he. No police record, well thought of by the local clergyman—he attends occasionally and when a boy was in the choir. During the Second World War he was an Air Raid Warden with a good record. At times he assisted the police in investigations."

It sounded too good to be true to Reed, who mistrusted people with a sense of public duty in the first place. Well thought of by the local clergyman! Reed snorted, then disguised the noise as a cough.

"Here is Peter Pipchin's address," Quant said pushing over two quarto sheets, "plus everything known about him. He was a family man, so you might go and see the widow. She drinks and I suppose I could authorise a bottle on your expenses."

Reed had inwardly winced at the address, a long grey street dating back three hundred years, never a territory of the rich as so many slums had once been, but always the haunt of the under-privileged and the have-nots, even in the days when the term ghetto applied only to the eminently civilised quarters of continental Jews. The Luftwaffe, Britain's foremost eraser of slum property, had missed it: and officialdom had not got round to demolishing its rows of grey houses, curiously beloved by their residents—*inmates*, thought Reed, might be a better word for them—for it was frequently by choice that people lived there.

He took a bottle of Scotch from the battered desk in the cubby-hole he shared with three other sergeants, scrutinised it to see that some ingenious colleague had not broached it and filled it up with water, as occasionally happened, put it in his brief-case and mooched forth. The hours before Opening Time were a trial to the Sergeant and people did tend to look at you if you used a hip flask even if you explained it was medicine. Nevertheless as he came out into Victoria Street he did pause and have a quick nip of rum, immediately feeling the odd pains in his legs disappear.

Beke Street had been last rebuilt by an eighteen-sixtyish builder who had died in an odour of sanctity with his only daughter married to a Scottish peer. He dismissed the taxi a hundred yards away. There was a sullenness about Beke Street, usually rather colourful, with women who looked like tarts but weren't, young men who dressed snappily, and older, grey-faced men with respiratory complaints and shabby clothes, old women with arthritis, and God alone knew how many children, all against the brooding façade of the terrace houses, the once whitened steps now the colour of mud.

When trouble struck Beke Street closed down. People in its two pubs whispered out of the side of their mouths. If a stranger asked a question there was blank silence and hostile stares. If you persisted it could be too bad for you. So it was now. The toddling children were off the streets. Only a few men, market traders mostly, were departing for work. Reed felt conspicuous, but that was all right. Policemen were safe enough in Beke Street when it was light.

He swisted the creaky old manual bell at number

sixty-nine. After doing this for a few minutes he kicked. In Beke Street you got the uneasy sensation of watching eyes, though if you swung round there was nobody at all.

The door was opened and Reed heard the heavy breathing before it fully opened. He was a big old man, completely bald, with three cardigans partly covering a shirt without a collar, anchored together by a large brass stud.

"Eff off," said the old man, wheezily.

"Police." Reed got his foot in the door.

He must have been a nasty customer in his day, thought Reed, before his lungs let him down. As it was he wheezed a little too long and the Sergeant squeezed halfway through the door.

"We 'ad you five o'clock this mornin'. Three of you." The old man sneered. "They still 'ave to come down Beke Street in threes. I remember when it was five and they was farting with fear all the way."

"Scotland Yard is where I come from, Dad," said Reed.

"I don't remember the woman," snarled the old man, "but I accept yer word for it."

"What about a drink?" said Reed. "I've got a bottle of Scotch in the bag. If you had a drop of milk, we could mix it. Nothing like it to line the stomach of a morning."

"This is a house of mourning," said the big old man, but wet his lips lickerishly.

"Perhaps I can come in for five minutes. Name of Reed, a Sergeant."

" 'Arry Joskin. Don't remember me, I s'pose. Nobody does, but I used to be a Strong Man in the circuses until my bowels started to trouble me. No good getting the trots when you are pulling seven men across the ring, *and* wearing tiger-skin tights. So I 'ad to reduce myself to the mindin' and chuckin' out until I got the pension. Ah, well, I'm Mrs. Pipchin's farver. 'E wasn't no loss rilly, but like these small men 'e 'ad an attraction for the women. She got to know that he weren't much cop, but of course she's in the kitchen 'owling like wimming do."

Seated in front of the kitchen sink in a rocking chair, looking vaguely at the china owl and alarm clock on the table, Mrs. Pipchin was drinking a large mug of tea, between loud hiccoughs. She looked about seventy, partly because she had not restored her dentures, partly because the women of Beke Street usually looked ten years older than their chronological age.

"Another copper, Eth," grunted Joskin.

" 'Ave they got the bugger wot done it?" enquired Mrs. Pipchin tearfully.

"It's early days, ma'am," said Reed, whipping the bottle out of his brief-case. "But what about a little of this in milk?"

Mr. Joskin, with a quickness that belied his age and bulk, had opened a grimy cupboard. Reed noticed four rusty, opened cans of herring in tomato sauce, the English delicacy in such parts. But there was an unopened bottle of milk.

The glasses looked greasy when Joskin produced them. Reed remembered that Jarvis with customary gloom always opined that infectious food-poisoning was an occupational disease, like fallen arches, and that danger money should liberally be paid.

Reed declined whisky himself, producing his hip flasp of rum. They drank for half an hour in silence, except that halfway through her first glass Mrs. Pipchin had observed "We don't know nothink", the classic formula of Beke Street.

"Any children, Mrs. P.?" asked the Sergeant after twenty-five minutes.

"Three boys, all in quad," answered Joskin, "and the girl who's 'oring up north."

"Can the boys be let out for the funeral?" enquired Mrs. Pipchin. "I meantersay the 'ole street 'll be at the funeral and the George and Crown afterwards and it would look bad if the boys weren't there. Young Maisie 'll read of it in the papers and come down to see her old mum. It was the Pakistanis that led 'er astray."

"I'll see what I can do," said Reed, "and there might be

89

twenty quid in it for you towards the wake." He tapped his breast pocket.

He drank companionably for the next quarter of an hour. Three-quarters of the whisky had gone and Joskin was weaving slightly as he rummaged for more milk.

"Twenty quid on that table?" asked Mrs. Pipchin.

Reed produced four five-pound notes and laid them down.

"Arter all he was my 'ubby," she said, wrestling with the obscure ethics of Beke Street. "Wotcher want?"

"Just a bit of background." Reed glanced about. "A fair earner, wasn't he?"

" 'E'd never work for less than a fiver a day," said Mrs. Pipchin. "Offer 'im four poun' ten and he'd spit on it. Trouble was he didn't work every day . . ."

"Did a bit of middleman work, didn't he?" suggested Reed.

"That's what 'e was. 'Lucky Alphonse, always in the middle', 'e used to quip. A merry man 'e was."

"Daft in his cups," said old Mr. Joskin, pouring.

"They all are," pronounced Mrs. Pipchin. "When the drink's in, the wit's out."

"Who was he generally working for?"

"We are not sayin' nothink," said the Relict, but drank with a certain relish.

"Old Dr. Dee and Fat used to use him," volunteered Joskin, ogling the Sergeant's rum flask.

"Barbados Navy Rum. Have a drop."

They both accepted.

"Goes down well after Scotch," said Mr. Joskin, sagely. "Mellers you, like."

Reed deliberately replaced the cover on the flask.

"We might as well tell 'im, Eth," said Mr. Joskin.

"Whatever you say, Dad."

"It was one Mr. Gaukroger, a business gentleman. Pete used to do a bit for him, going between in buying things. They'd put the price up on, say, a thousand Army blankets if they saw Mr. Gaukroger in 'is Bentley, but with Peter, with only half an arsepiece in his trousers so to speak, they was reasonable if the greasy notes was there on the barrel, so to speak", said Mr. Joskin.

"What was he doing this time?"

"The day before he died," Mrs. Pipchin belched and absent-mindedly reached forward and grabbed the flask, "and I mus' say"—eyeing her father with a certain amount of belligerence—"that Peter never went out of this 'ouse wivout hall the buttons on 'is fly; *and* his arsepiece sewn up. Sometimes patched, that I can't deny 'aving known hard times, but always decent."

"It was only so to speak," said Mr. Joskin placatingly. "You always kept 'im decent and his shoes shone."

"The day before he died," soothed Reed.

"He said that he had a job for Gaukroger," confided Mrs. Pipchin. "A nasty little job, which he had demanded eight quid to do. Mr. Gaukroger is a hard man, but he gave poor Peter four nicker in advance and two quid for taxis."

"I suppose he went out late at night?"

"About ten he went," said Mrs. Pipchin. "He was goin' to get the bus and then walk to save a few bob, but he said he'd get a taxi back and I could expect him around three. As it was I was fast asleep and it was eight o'clock when I got up to make the breakfast that I see the bed's empty."

"You were worried?"

"I knew it weren't a dame. I gave 'im, poor soul, a dose with a port bottle and didn't use the label side, about twenty years ago when I caught him with a neighbour and 'e 'ad been faithful ever since because Dad promised to break his back if I complained. He was only a *little* man. Anyway in his line of country you sometimes don't come 'ome for several days. Somethink with money in it happens. Once he was away three weeks and then turns up with five 'undred quid. They'd knocked off a country 'ouse, got panicky and employed little Pete to take the plunder to the fence. No 'arm in saying that now 'e's gone."

"What was he doing for Mr. Gaukroger?"

"He wasn't one for talking," said Mrs. Pipchin, "but he did say he was arranging the collection of some money that was owing to Mr. Gaukroger. I said, 'No trouble, I hope'. Peter said, 'Just a matter of arranging for the collection, dearie'."

Sergeant Reed thanked them, noticing that the pubs were by then just opening. In one of them he obtained a rum to strengthen his stomach muscles and leisurely made his way back to report to Superintendent Quant.

"We can't put the inquest off indefinitely," sighed Quant, "though we'll try for an adjournment. It'll be a field-day for the press, two murders in one pub. I do wish we had some sensible form of censorship to stop them putting ideas into people's heads. Mark my words, there will be other killings in pubs for a time. Like those dirty books I have been reading, putting fornication into people's heads."

"It's a natural thought," said Reed, glowing with rum.

"Not with me," said Quant, "and never has been. And I won't promote any man who I think dwells on it. Ah, well, it's a sad, sinful world, and Harry Alwyn must have killed Peter Pipchin. We must find who the third man is. The Brewery has complained to the Home Secretary already and unfortunately alcohol is a major source of revenue. How can we increase the taxation if we allow people to be killed in public houses, they ask? The Prime Minister is worried. This Gaukroger seems a wheeler-dealer, but that type only comes up for embezzlement, false pretences and the like. The mother-in-law is a different kettle of fish. Her pa, almost before your time, was the biggest jewellery fence we ever saw and a dangerous man to boot."

"Shall I look up Gaukroger? He has his office in The Poultry," said Reed.

"Do that," said Quant dismally. "I have to report to the Commander and Whitehall is worried about underground films again. The Prime Minister can't understand why they are not healthy, about yachts and things like that. For years" —the old Superintendent groaned like a sepulchre—"they

92

thought they were about the underground railway, but then a couple of M.P.s saw some of them in a night club. Why can't people be reasonable, Mr. Reed? We only ask them to abstain from excess!"

"Human nature," said Reed as he stood up to go.

"We must fight it." The Superintendent straightened his bowed back and sounded firm.

Reg Gaukroger, said the chaste gold-painted inscription over the false agate wall of the smart new office block. Three rooms, thought Reed from experience. Master, accountant plus assistant, and typist cum filing clerk. It was deceptive. A great deal of business could be done with such a set-up. He knocked at the door and a judas window slid open to reveal an unpleasant female face adorned by the sharpest and beadiest eyes that Reed had seen for some time.

"Have you an appointment?" It was an educated voice.

"Metropolitan Police. Sergeant Reed by name." He wished he was in a quiet pub eating steak-and-kidney pie.

"Your warrant?"

Reed fumbled, then brandished it.

"I'll see whether he's in."

"I can wait all day," said Reed laconically.

The window slammed shut.

Five minutes passed and the door opened grudgingly. "Mr. Gaukroger will see you."

Reg Gaukroger, smooth, shaven, eupeptic and slightly vulgar, presided behind a clean desk with two telephones.

He eyed Reed with practised shrewdness. "Is it about the camping gear, Sergeant? I explained that to an Inspector yesterday. I sold it lock, stock and barrel the day after acquiring it. All in good faith."

"A Peter Pipchin has been found dead," said the Sergeant, flatly. "His wife says he was on an errand for you to the Admiral Byng public house. It was murder."

Gaukroger was a cool man, thought Reed.

93

"Pipchin used to work for me as a debt collector," said Gaukroger. "Alwyn owed me money. I asked Pipchin to give him a message that I'd like what was outstanding paid back."

"How much?"

"That I am not prepared to divulge. Nor have you the right to ask." Gaukroger was blustering slightly.

"The Coroner could ask you at the inquest, you know. Not that we wish to call upon innocent bystanders and expose them to publicity."

Gaukroger produced a cigar and a cutter and operated. His face, decided Reed, was one that rather demanded a cigar. He noted that it was Cuban, of the kind imported via Berlin if you had the connections.

Finally Gaukroger said, "He was a good friend of my wife and her mother. For that reason I did not wish to approach him directly. It was a matter of twelve hundred pounds. Money is tight at the moment and I could do with it."

"Have you a receipt?" asked Reed sceptically.

"No receipt," said Gaukroger. "It was a gents' agreement."

"I hope you pulled the plug," said Reed.

"Now, look here," said Gaukroger, "if we can't discuss this reasonably I don't want to discuss it at all."

"Did you know that Alwyn received stolen property?"

Gaukroger pursed his mouth. "I'll be frank with you, Sergeant, I would not have been surprised. For the simple reason that I'm a dealer and as you know you meet funny people in that trade. I keep my hands clean, but there we are, that's a frank admission."

"I am not running a French cinema"—Reed had wind generated by an empty stomach and was in no mood to be polite.

"I'd have no reason at all to murder Pipchin," protested Gaukroger. "He was just a busy little man you could hire

94

for a fiver a day. We all do it, us dealers, because if we roll up in the big cars the price gets higher."

"We have reason to believe that Harry Alwyn dealt in stolen property," said Reed stubbornly.

"My books are open to scrutiny," said Gaukroger, "and are properly audited. I buy and I sell, but the stuff is rigidly legitimate, no question of that. For instance," he donned spectacles and stared at a notebook, "this morning I was notified that they had made one hundred and twenty thousand sets of tropical underwear for East of Suez, but by mistake they made them for ladies. The very thing for a summer holiday on the Costa. I tendered thirty new pence per set. I will resell them at forty-five. That is my business, Government Disposal Sales! They will do it! You are too young to remember the Slough Dump, but the dealers made the big money out of it."

CHAPTER FOUR

"LADIES' TROPICAL UNDERWEAR," said the Commander dismally at the four o'clock conference. "I checked the War Office and they did have them made. The politician who drew up the plans apparently wears ladies' combinations. It was merely to check Gaukroger's credibility gap which seems to be zero. I suggest as a hypothesis that Alwyn did owe him money and that he sent Pipchin to collect, it being ungentlemanly to ask your wife's lover to refund cash. At the pub Pipchin encountered the killer who did him in."

"There are rumours," said Inspector Booker, "of a lot of hot money about. That might mean that the late Alwyn fenced the bank loot and was killed in a quarrel concerning the spoils."

"Mrs. Stoney," said Sergeant Jarvis, "is Gaukroger's mother-in-law and a hard-faced old bitch from an old criminal family. Suppose Gaukroger turns 'black' money into 'white'?"

"It could be," said the Commander. "Gaukroger works on small margins by all accounts. When you change illicit money the margin does not matter that much as long as you get the cash value back."

"Mrs. Stoney," said a quiet, grizzled old Inspector in the corner, "has retired to her home in Dorset. The funny thing is that she always does this if things get hot. It is difficult to observe her, her house being in an obscure village named Blakeley. Nothing there, not even the local police station, which was closed three years ago. You could open the one-man station, it's still on the books, with a bedroom and a kitchen cum bathroom."

"Humphrey," said the Commander swiftly, "I will get

on to the local Chief Constable and you will open the Blakeley Station. What is the address?"

"Twelve, Squeeze Belly Passage," said the Inspector. "A very narrow-streeted town of small alleys."

"I hope you will not abuse your trust," said the Commander severely to Humphrey. "Retreat before young women with busts!"

"Yes, sir."

"It's mostly butchers," said the old Inspector, "the slaughter yard being off it. Butchers aren't fussy as a rule. But mind the fact that they often carry knives attached to their belts. I knew of an unfortunate case on an underground train in the rush hour."

"If Sergeant Humphrey is injured in Squeeze Belly Passage," said the Commander, "it will be in the line of duty and pensionable. But as a cover it should be ideal : find out about the lady, visit the house on some pretext!"

"I'll get my overnight bag," said Humphrey and presently took a cab to Paddington Station.

Historically Blakeley was one of the ruins which Oliver Cromwell knocked about a bit, and nothing apparently had been done to remedy his depredations except some loathsome Victorian red-brick and rows of houses erected after the First World War for returning heroes which by now were falling down. There were four pubs and a fish-and-chip shop and a police inspector of curdled and depressive nature.

"I had a call from the Commander," he said through an odour of beer. "I had the old station in Squeeze Belly Passage duly cleaned, the bill to your expense. Mrs. Stoney has her house and rose garden a quarter of a mile away and for your edification she is a fornicating old bitch of the first water. Seven months ago, if you please, the cook reported that the house had been burgled. Mrs. S. has two servants, a cook and a chauffeur. There are elaborate burglar alarms.

97

I went there myself, and if there *was* a burglary it was an inside job with a door key used. Abusive she was and wrote to the local M.P. You know what that means, all the ruddy writing up of 'please explain' reports. Something fishy there, I'll be bound."

At this hour the Sergeant was thinking rather wistfully of the local fish-and-chip shop, but he said, "I could purport to be pursuing the crime, sir."

"She was cagey," said the Inspector. "She alleged that a small trunk had been taken, but she said there was just miscellaneous paper in it. At first I suspected an insurance fraud, now I don't know. London told me she comes of a criminal family, so perhaps it is hijacking."

"I'd better settle into Squeeze Belly Passage," said Humphrey dismally.

"A ghastly place," said the Inspector, "though there is one small gas heater in the office which apparently works. The Commander said there had been two murders which this hag might have knowledge of."

The best the Inspector could do in the way of transport, the economy drive being what it is, was a large rusty bicycle, of 1920 vintage, and upon this monster Sergeant Humphrey set out for Squeeze Belly Passage with the keys of the police sub-station. He had to dismount from the machine at the end of the narrow alley and push it, barking one shin against a pedal. It was a darkish, dismal thoroughfare, apparently some kind of easement between ruined, desolated and abandoned warehouses. Faintly Humphrey could hear the shrieking of pigs being manhandled in the local slaughter-house. Halfway along, where the Passage jinked to the right he encountered a sturdy old lady wearing a cap and carrying a sack. Groaningly he prepared to back.

"Don't worry, just let me toss the sack of lights over first," which she promptly did. "Now get against the wall wiv yer bike."

This Humphrey did and the lady, an old hand apparently, swarmed over the machine successfully, though giving the

Sergeant a painful blow in the pit of the stomach *en route*.

"You'll get used to it, duck," she called back.

The police sub-station was a runtish building standing between warehouses. It smelled of ancient socks. Downstairs was a room with a battered desk, two chairs, gas fire of minuscule proportions which uttered peculiar belching sounds when lit. Behind was a bedroom, and true to his word the Inspector had had it furbished with what looked like old prison blankets and caused the enormous chamber pot to be polished and placed at the ready. The electric bulbs, devoid of shades, were of the lowest possible wattage, and from the small kitchen, plainly unused for thirty years, he recoiled. He never found the nerve to traverse the rickety stairs to find out what was above them—a gallows perhaps, he thought with gloom.

There was only one thing to do, so leaving the bike propped against the desk he went to the nearest pub, at the further end of the Passage which eventually descended upon a depressing-looking residential area. Here he announced to an interested publican that he was the new Sergeant stationed in Squeeze Belly Passage, and arranged to take temporary board on a daily basis.

The Inspector had told the Sergeant with gloomy relish that the weather was about to take a turn for the worse and that the state of it in Blakeley was notoriously the worst in southern England. Sure enough, when he woke up next morning Humphrey saw the sleet drifting before the window of a freezing bedroom. He dubiously dabbed himself in a bathroom which appeared not to have been used for some time and went down to over-fried bacon and leathery egg. He sometimes wished that his mother had not made him promise never to drink before noon, his father having had that distressing habit. He had spent the previous evening at darts with gregarious and garrulous locals, by whom he

99

hoped that the news of a new appointment to Squeeze Belly Passage would rapidly be disseminated.

Mrs. Stoney, he had no trouble in ascertaining, lived in a house with half an acre of ground called The Acacias. It was pleasantly Georgian with six bedrooms and modernised plumbing. Reluctantly he donned his thick raincoat, wished that he had waterproof gaiters, and walked back to his office where mercifully the state of the weather was concealed by the dirt covering the small windows. He used his electric shaver and read the paper—the weather forecast spoke of the coldest winter for fifty years—until ten o'clock when he wheeled the old bike out. The sleet had finished and it was warmer, though leaden skies framed the grimy silhouettes of the old warehouses. He consulted the possibly inaccurate map that the publican had drawn for him and set off for The Acacias. His cover story was that the authorities had become alarmed at vandalism committed upon old, historic houses— he instanced several imaginary cases.

"Those university buggers!" had snarled the publican. "Why my 'ard-earned money goes to support 'em in luxury when they should be 'orse-whipped or 'anged is more than mortal man can tell."

The bike had demonstrably never been oiled and the Sergeant's riding muscles ached from the previous evening, but eventually he found himself pushing the machine up the gravelled drive of The Acacias. A forbidding, close-trapped harridan answered his ring and peered at him. She wore a uniform and an expression of sly malignity.

"I'm the local police Sergeant."

"Oh, I say." She had a Cockney accent.

"I would like to see the lady of the house," persisted Humphrey.

"She wouldn't degrade 'erself by seeing no Sergeant," said the harridan. "Get the Superintendent to come along and she'll give 'im a few minutes."

"It's in her interest that I should see her. She won't be pleased if I don't see her."

For a moment the woman hesitated, then grudgingly allowed him in.

Mrs. Stoney, her yellow hair in pins and her face wrinkled, was consuming prawns and drinking gin out of an expensive-looking glass. Her living-room had a rather false elegance as had the lady herself.

"What's this about?" she said sharply.

"I'm the local Sergeant in Squeeze Belly Passage. It's vandalism, ma'am. They go round beating up historical old houses, little gems of our history."

"My late father always said that the Americans should have dropped the bomb on the Russians instead of those nice little Japs," said Mrs. Stoney, cryptically. She was, realised the Sergeant, a little tight. People like Mrs. Stoney were never tight at this hour except when under exceptional strain.

"I believe you had a robbery some time ago, ma'am."

"And had a pompous Inspector here who did nothing." Humphrey noticed that Mrs. Stoney's china-blue eyes were very hard under the mascara.

"What did you lose?" Humphrey wheedled.

"A trunk with newspapers in it."

"Valuable, were they?"

"They were placed inside to keep the ants out."

"I suppose," said Humphrey, "that you had no idea who did it?"

"I told the imbecile Inspector that I had not." Mrs. Stoney was very short and she was looking carefully up at the Sergeant. "Haven't I seen you before?"

"I have been around Blakeley for some time."

Humphrey had the feeling that she did not believe him, so he thanked her and went, escorted by the harridan. On the way he noticed a black-haired man polishing some brasswork. He did not like the look of him.

He went to see the dismal Inspector. "I think she smelled a very big rat," he said. "She is a cunning old lady, wouldn't you say?"

"Cunning is an understatement." The Inspector had been eating garlic sausage.

"If there is any loot at The Acacias, she'll move it right smartly." Humphrey put out the bait and the Inspector measured his personal dislike of Mrs. Stoney against the inevitable queries from the district auditor.

"Complete surveillance," he said gloomily.

"The staff look to me as though they might have records," said Humphrey.

"She brings them down from London," said the Inspector, fiddling a bit of sausage from his front teeth. "A hag who is housemaid and cook and a black-haired man with a mashed snout who is chauffeur cum useful. I never have got a line on them, not that I have had any real reason to. They don't go out of the house except sometimes to shop and have no communication with the locals."

"The man might be tough."

"I've got a few tough boys on the staff," said the Inspector. "We sometimes get kids from London and they don't like the medicine they are given."

"I'd like to lend a hand," said Humphrey.

"There is only one way out of The Acacias," said the Inspector, "and that is on to the main road. I keep a record of entrances because it saves time in burglary cases. Over the road is a smallholding where I'll put a man with a walkie-talkie. I'll have two vans, with three men in each, strategically placed. Not," he added, "that anything will probably happen."

It started to hail at four o'clock in the morning. Sergeant Humphrey, behind a hedge with two constables, was steadily drenched. Fortunately the elder constable, a philosophical man, had provided himself with the official flask of brandy reserved for accident cases and passed it round.

There came a light at The Acacias. "That's 'er car," said

the elder constable as a Mercedes came out. He talked into the head-set.

Eventually they got into a van. Mrs. Stoney's car was driven cunningly and professionally, but the police driver was a match. Peering through the windscreen Humphrey did not think they could have been spotted.

A scant three miles away was an old canal, with steps leading down to the waterway. The police driver passed as the Mercedes stopped.

A hundred yards further on they stopped.

"There's a path down," muttered the elderly constable. "We'd better be nippy, 'cause they're going to chuck summit into the drink."

Humphrey, his feet precariously seeking the way in the darkness, led the way. There was a frightened squeak as he flushed out an avidly courting couple who fled past them. He cursed under his breath, and the rain dripped down his neck.

On the canal bank he ordered the flashlights to be turned on and through the haze saw the black-haired male servitor of Mrs. Stoney, accompanied by the harridan, carrying a black tin box between them. The elderly constable was surprisingly nippy on his feet and pushing Humphrey aside sprinted up and gave the harridan a swift blow in the stomach.

" 'Ere," said the black-jowled man, aghast, "you're hitting a woman." Profiting by his moral attitude, the other constable hit him under the jaw while Humphrey damply sat on the tin box.

From there on it was routine and the local police station.

The dismal Inspector supervised the forcing open of the tin box. It was full of five-pound notes which when carefully counted totalled thirty-five thousand pounds.

"Any explanation?" asked the Inspector, but the man and the woman remained silent.

"Get Mrs. Stoney on the blower," ordered the Inspector, but there was no reply to the repeated ringing.

"Put them in the cells," said the Inspector, "that'll be all for tonight." He eyed Humphrey with the evident suspicion that the unfortunate young man was entirely responsible for his absence from the nuptial bed.

As a result Humphrey found himself in the heavy rain without transport. He walked back to Squeeze Belly Passage and let himself into the police station.

The gas fire groaned and wheezed as he lit it. Always on the hypochondriac side—his mother had carried on about his weak chest—Humphrey divested himself of his clothes and placed them on the rickety chair in front of the gas fire. He found the old, greasy towel and wiped his wet pelt with it. There was a flurried knocking at the front door and absent-mindedly he opened it.

Through the blur of rain he saw a little old lady with steel-rimmed glasses who piped: "Oh, Mr. Policeman, my pussy has completely disappeared!"

With a faint howl of terror, Humphrey held the hand towel in front of him in the attitude of an apprentice matador attempting a veronica.

"Sometimes I think I can hear him miaowing," said the old lady helpfully.

The penny dropped. "Eke," she said and disappeared into Squeeze Belly Passage.

Humphrey decided to risk the horrors of the police-station bed and lay there listening to the rain.

Superintendent Quant was in a bad mood the following morning. There lay on his desk a report claiming that Sergeant Humphrey might have been guilty of indecent exposure and his old squeaky fountain pen made the necessary annotation on the Sergeant's personal file, 'No further promotion in view of his sexual propensities'. The local Inspector at Blakeley had been upbraided by his wife for keeping late hours and had not spared Humphrey in his report.

Groaning, the old Superintendent made his way to the mid-day conference.

Inspector Booker led off, "The notes, from samples examined, are counterfeit and not good ones. Probably of Belgian origin and meant for the tourist trade. You can get stung very easily trading in currency in Brussels. As to Mrs. Stoney, who is now back in London, she denies all knowledge. It is no offence to possess false currency. The offence is to utter. This she has not done. You know, gentlemen, that it is possible that Harry Alwyn sold the stolen notes several times, substituting counterfeit. That would provide a pretty good motive for murder."

Reed got up next. "Alwyn had been staying in mostly," he said. "And the pub was up for sale. There is a man named Pudding, a brewery representative who I had a drink with yesterday. I got it out of him in strict confidence, the brewery not liking their affairs discussed. I agree with the Inspector that Alwyn had been selling forged notes under the guise of being genuine, stolen ones and that this in all probability was the motive for the killing in some way or another. He may have taken a dead liberty with some Mafia type of gang. Nevertheless the pub was a very safe place. It is difficult to kill anybody during opening hours—too many witnesses—and at night he would be locked in his room, which has a telephone extension—*unless he was expecting somebody he trusted*."

The Commander had been scratching his head. "I do not like the association of Mrs. Stoney and the Gaukrogers with Alwyn." What to do, thought the Commander. Mrs. Stoney seemed a hardened, close-trapped old crook. The weakest link might be Mrs. Gaukroger, particularly as she had been Harry Alwyn's mistress. Sergeant Humphrey was an obvious choice, thought the Commander, a lusty boy but by report a sex maniac. One had to be so careful. Inspector Booker was a walking compendium of information but had a selection of warts on his face and his sex-appeal rating was zero. Jarvis? It did not appear that Mrs. Gaukroger would be greatly interested in varicose veins. Which, the work schedule being what it was, left Reed. The cherubic, drunken Sergeant had an attraction for women sometimes. They wished to reform him, a female vice for which they often paid dearly. He made the decision.

"Sergeant Reed," said the Commander, "get close to Mrs. Gaukroger."

CHAPTER FIVE

T H E L A D Y W A S at home. Reed, huddled in his thickest coat, was admitted to the penthouse smelling of gin. The Gaukrogers possessed a sly-looking male factotum who answered the door.

"Regarding Mr. Alwyn," he said to the elegant-looking lady upon the very expensive-looking settee, "I'm looking into his death."

"Why question me?" Her voice was ice-cold.

"Now, my dear," said the Sergeant, "perhaps I could sit down and discuss the business nice and cosy. There is no point in being nasty because we know quite a lot and can guess more."

She gave a sudden, sad little gamin grin. "I suppose, as you smell of it so much, you could do with a gin. And take your coat off or you'll catch your death when you go out."

The factotum served and Mrs. Gaukroger took a small gin and a piece of terrine.

"There were police here the other night," observed Mrs. Gaukroger. "A handsome young man and an older type who harangued my mother about piles. He seemed to suffer from every known ailment. My mother is something of a hypochondriac and he much impressed her."

"Now, me dear," said the Sergeant, "let us have no witty remarks. Who killed poor Harry Alwyn?"

Mrs. Gaukroger started to cry.

"Have a drop of gin," said the Sergeant, getting up and seizing the bottle. "Nothing like it to steady the nerves and dry the tears."

Mrs. Gaukroger drank while the Sergeant watched clinically. There is a crucial point with gin whereupon the imbiber starts to talk.

"I loved him," she said, simply.

"A marriage of convenience between you and Gaukroger?"

"Yes."

"I suppose Mr. Gaukroger turns the black money into white."

She drained her gin and Reed poured again.

"I don't think I should say anything."

"Put it this way," said Reed, "and it's an old, old story. Crooks accumulate money and goods, but the crunch comes from the income-tax boys. 'Where did you get the money to buy that car' stuff. So the only thing is to set up an honest business and trade at a loss. What the residue is becomes honest money."

"My mother," said Mrs. Gaukroger, belching slightly but pouring another gin, "is the brains behind my husband. He does not have many apart from book-keeping. But Reg did not kill Harry Alwyn. Reg has not the nerve to kill *anyone*."

"Harry was planning to get out, was he not?" said Reed rather brutally.

"We had *both* had it," she said. "We were going off together. Harry was making his final deal and thereafter it was me and him in the sun. He thought maybe north of Brisbane where you can lie in the sun all the day."

"I suppose he sold your mother some notes?"

"They were stolen from my mother. Her house was broken into and the trunkful taken. One of the servants made the mistake of phoning the police."

"But she got them back."

"Harry arranged it with the thieves. My mother paid another two thousand pounds."

Lying like hell, thought Reed. She had obviously been in the scheme to rook Mama. The old lady was probably good for another twenty years and Mrs. Gaukroger wanted her share now . . .

"Where did these notes come from?" he asked.

She shrugged prettily and poured another gin for them both.

"Did your mother know the notes were part of a bank robbery?"

Mrs. Gaukroger looked cunning, her rather small face twisting sideways.

"But she didn't buy the notes, ducky, the notes were snide. No harm in possessing them if you don't try to *pass* them."

"Did Harry Alwyn have the originals?"

"I suppose there is no harm saying it now. He did. They were going cheap because they thought the numbers had been taken, but somebody assured Harry that it was not so. He bought them from a man in Liverpool for five thousand pounds."

"Who assured him?"

"Ducky, we never talked about that. Live and let live was our motto."

"Did you know a Peter Pipchin?"

"Mr. Gaukroger, I think but without being sure, used to employ him as a debt collector."

"He was killed at the Admiral Byng."

"My God!" She went white.

"Have another gin," said the Sergeant comfortably. "And don't worry your pretty little head about it. Lord, there are corpses everywhere in my business."

"Harry was not a killer," she said. "And if we put the cards on the table it was not a matter of scruples. He just could never see a percentage in violence. Harry liked a bit off the top of the milk bottle. He'd come to the end of the road, as you often do. His nerve was failing him at times and that was fatal in his business, so he wanted out in a big way. And it was the final killing that he planned." She stopped as though aghast at her own words.

"So who killed him?" asked Reed.

"He knew so many crooks, some violent. Do you know Dr. Dee?"

"Yes."

"He makes me shudder, but he would have you killed without dropping a tear."

"Harry dealt with him?"

"Harry was his agent," she said. "Sometimes it was stuff going out of the country, sometimes loot coming in. Mind you, I think Harry was going to sell the real notes to the old Doctor. Harry was more than a bit afraid of him, a foreigner, my dearie, and you cannot trust them with a knife, all that communism inside them as Reg says. Most of the boys that Harry dealt with haven't got really effective contacts outside the U.K., but the Doctor has. He can get you kicked to death from Capri to Cracow, and from what I've been told about the bastard he's probably got an in with the Russians as well. That's why poor Harry and me chose Queensland, where the Mafia is third generation and very snobbish about the European and American lot and the police don't bother you if you know the right people. Just lie in the sun, dear, that's what we were going to do apart from shooting crocodiles. I'd like to shoot a crocodile because they remind me of darling Mummy. Shooting them in their big mouth is best, so Harry used to say."

Reed freshened his drink. His head was knocking and he abhorred the no-man's-land between the borders of comparative sobriety and comparative inebriation, when he thought best.

"Funny you not minding Alwyn jobbin' your mum, not to mention your lawful wedded hubby," he said dully.

"Gaukroger is Mum's puppet. In some ways he is rather a sweet, not but that a little of him doesn't go an awful long way. But he's done all right out of us. Reg will always have his six thou a year from the property he's bought, even if he is looking out of a cell window at it. If it hadn't been for Mum Reg would be cost accountant in a sausage factory, a very good, clean and obliging one, mind you."

"And Mum?"

"I didn't know Grandpa much," said Mrs. Gaukroger. "He didn't like kids except, I guess, my mother and even then he regarded her more as a son than as a daughter. She married according to his wishes. My father was a dish among dishes, you've no idea just how fascinating, and about five years the younger. It was one of Grandpa's few mistakes. Father had the lot except . . . except guts and besides being a woman-chaser he was dumb enough to boast about it so that it got back to Mother and Grandpa. He was running the bookie business quite successfully when all the trouble started. I was away at school. He used to write, pathetic letters really because underneath he was terrified. Finally he bolted to Australia—funny that Harry and I were to do the same thing, though it is about the only place to bolt to nowadays, Canada being so cold and given to kidnapping and the Afros likely to turn so funny."

"His record sheet seems to have been a violent one as far as Australia is concerned, I scanned his Interpol sheet."

"It was weakness, I think. To screw himself up he had to take a bit of jam, you know, a white sniff. Then, of course, he didn't know what he was doing for an hour."

"You know a lot," said Reed. He was feeling more queasy and the central heating was oppressive. It was impossible in these MGM surroundings, what with the bathrooms, extractor fans, and deodorant drenchings, but he could have sworn to a whiff of old armpits.

"You can't touch bitch and not be defiled," Mrs. Gaukroger smirked merrily, "and not to put too fine a point on it my mum and her friends are a proper lot of old bitches. They are Relicts, love, of the most dangerous crooks in London. Women all outlive men, have a look at Worthing. Something to do with the thick stuff that forms in the arteries. After all the men have to do the stuff like bashing and getting in windows which plays hell with their guts."

It was true, thought Reed gloomily. London was filled with elderly ladies whose husbands had knocked themselves out in the pursuit of dishonest cash.

There *were* villains who felt no tension, most con men as it happened. Reed thought that they were so skilled at weaving fantasies that they always had their private little door through which they could disappear at will, like the rangy, suntanned 'ex-captain' he had pulled in a month previously. In his more eupeptic phases, wearing the medals he had acquired in the Congo, some of them quite remarkably coloured, he appeared actually to believe that the blocks of land in Spain he was flogging existed. But the other boys invariably wound up with spastic colons, fits of painful retching, palpitating hearts and increasing reliance on the little bottles of Swiss-manufactured pills. One of these days the Welfare State would recognise the fact and stick five per cent on income tax to provide special clinics. Reed sat there polishing his nails against his thighs, noticing that gin and emotion had made Mrs. Gaukroger's make-up run.

"When I was four I knew that a fence wasn't something you just bounced a ball against," gloomed his hostess, rucking down her midi—about sixty quid's worth of it, thought the Sergeant and wondered if the dress had been stolen, a lot having gone off lately. "Grandpa was self-made. His mum was a widow-lady, one of the last of the tally ladies who worked the big houses around London in the eighteen seventies, I guess it was. She had a head on her—just a penny in the shilling each week while you were paying off a super new bonnet costing two and threepence. Of course Great-grandma was able to figure and they weren't, poor things, some of them getting two bob a week and live in, and sooner or later they owed her more than they earned. So then came the c-r-u-n-c-h: perhaps the maid, or cook or what-have-you, had something which would do in lieu of cash. A lot of things used to be lying around in those great rambling places where nothing was ever thrown away. Great-gran never carried away the hot stuff, that was her son's job and he became pretty adept at it. I once heard him tell Mum that he often carried as much as six pounds in silver articles after a good month of trolling. Then there was the 'key to the cellar-door' caper. It was always off the stone landing at the bottom of the area steps. It was the best way to get in, with a horse and cart waiting to take the loot away. Great-grandma could always con, threaten or bribe somebody to give her a lend of the key for five minutes. She was a thorough woman who'd have been a Labour M.P. today, bless her, and she had Grandpa taught by a locksmith how to take an impression. Oh, the old lady took no part in the actual smashing, she just set the thing up and sold the info plus a key for ten pound to one or other of the Deptford gangs."

A regular little encyclopaedia of crime, thought Reed. The housebreaking gangs had holed up in Deptford in the fog-ridden last decades of Victoria's reign, the reason being that it was outside the jurisdiction of the Metropolitan Police and on the periphery of the somnolent Kentish Constabulary. Christ! They even had Chris Marlowe knocked off in a knocking-shop there, the chivving being whitewashed by one of the notorious Kent Coroners. Reed's now bleary brain started to miss names. Marlowe had lived when another lady was Queen . . . who was she?

"Another gin, love?" Mrs. Gaukroger, her eyes now dry, had refilled his glass. It tasted sweetish. "Grandad started the bookie bit on the way," she said. "A lot of people— some of them the well-to-do types who had their own drinking cupboards, others just betting in pennies—could not get a bet on easily. You could put paper money in an envelope and send it to a Swiss bookie, but if the bet won most often he just threw envelope, money and betting slip into the fire, like the Swiss still do, love, only a bit different. So Grandpa, first in a small way . . ."

But like a bit of sodden driftwood, the Sergeant had fallen forward on his chair so that his chest pressed on her feet. Mrs. Gaukroger felt for her tissues and repaired her face. It was funny, she thought, how the writers insisted that the knock-out drops hit you suddenly after violent movement. Really you just sank down a nice warm pit of sludge.

She raised her voice. "Charlie!"

Had Reed looked closely at the manservant he might have observed a certain toughness under the sleek exterior.

"Used the old drops, did you?" he said as he gazed at the Sergeant's face.

"You couldn't get him drunk, not really. He was full, or so I thought, when he came, but the way he was guzzling away at the gin it would have been me who passed out first."

"You look half shickered, love," said Charlie.

"I'll be right when I've been sick," said Mrs. Gaukroger, for she had that useful talent.

"You sung to him nicely," said Charles with a glance at the service hatch in the corner.

It was a pity that he had not many brains, thought Mrs. Gaukroger. Her husband employed him in the role of occasional bodyguard, generally discreet factotum and a man who could act as manservant when there were guests. If pressed concerning the last accomplishment Charles would rightly say that he had been in charge of the waiting staff in an officers' mess, omitting the fact that the officers were prison officers and that he himself was serving the last two of a five-year sentence.

"You should not listen so much through the servery," she said, rather unconvincingly for she had the feeling that Charles, if manipulated correctly, might be a comfort to her. She squirmed to her feet and Sergeant Reed rolled sideways on to the floor with a sacklike thud. His face was a white mask etched by the drink-ruptured capillaries. They always looked like that, but Mrs. Gaukroger felt prematurely queasy. However, Charles, bending, was feeling the Sergeant's pulse.

"You can't acksherly kill a drunken pisspot," he observed. "They always crawl through. My dad was a seaman and he used to get the drops in every whorehouse on the China run —never learned—but he's eighty and does a bit of pimping on the side to stretch the Old Age Pension and what he wheedles out of the Good Samaritans Mission to Seamen. And talk about drink! But look here, what are we goin' to *do* with this. He'll be out for how long?"

"I gave him the four-hour dose," said Mrs. Gaukroger, sullenly because her head was aching.

"That means he'll be stirring around six," said Charlie, "and in a ripe bad temper. A nasty time of the day to have trouble with everybody on their way home. And what will Mr. G. say?"

"He's spending the evening at the Society of Chartered Accountants."

Charlie allowed himself the benefit of a small guffaw at the euphemism, for both of them knew that Mr. Gaukroger's Thursday nights were spent with a plump blonde lady at Richmond who could be chartered, undoubtedly could account, but was hardly society.

Yet they would have to do something with him, thought Mrs. Gaukroger. The Sergeant was too experienced a soak to be cajoled into believing that he had in reality passed out from drink. It had sometimes occurred to her that a penthouse with a patio and a rather low balustrade might provide a solution from an oppressive circumstance, but she thought that in these meddlesome days all sorts of tests might be carried out at the dictate of the Coroner. She forced herself to think. "The service lift," she said at last.

"And fourteen stone odd of him," said Charlie. "He mustn't be damaged, as dragging might, for that can mean very bad trouble. P'raps you could take his feet. The lift won't be wanted much at this hour, but you can see into it as it passes the floors on account of the fact that the door is an open grill. Still, we might sort of prop him up and pretend to be talking. Then there is the delivery yard. I could back the car into it."

Mrs. Gaukroger ran a largish estate car, against her inclinations but at her mother's advice. "You can get things *into* an estate car, dear," Mrs. Stoney had pontificated, "and you never know. Your sainted grandpa always had two drivers on hand with trucks just in case of eventualities." Reluctantly at the time Mrs. Gaukroger had abandoned something small and sporty because she recognised Mummy's long experience in such matters. Now it would be a godsend.

"There's a man," said Charlie, "an assistant janitor, who

has a shed down there and looks after the garbage, bottles and sanitary traps. Old Ted is his name. He doesn't half pong, upon my oath."

Mrs. Gaukroger was feeling decidedly ill, but steeled herself. "Does he bet?"

"Of course."

"Send the old fool to the nearest betting shop with a fiver and a list of horses. Tell him he's on to a free drink anyway and ten per cent of the winnings."

"What horses?" Wheezing slightly Charlie had hefted Reed into an easy chair and was taking a medicinal swig from the gin bottle. There had been a time when Charlie could—and did—shin up drainpipes with the best of them, but the years of stodgy prison fare and a sedentary occupation had made him go somewhat in the wind.

Mrs. Gaukroger momentarily raised her pale eyes to the ceiling. She thought she might be very sick indeed and the light pouring in from the huge glass windows seemed suffused with small, black dancing shapes.

"Pick three or four out of the newspaper, any horses," she managed to say.

"National Hunt has been abandoned due to the frozen ground what is too hard for their legs, 'orses' gams being so skinny when you look at them close. Old Ted is not very bright but would smell horse manure if you sent him off on that lurk."

"The pub, then, send him to buy a bottle of Scotch and give him a bit over for a drink."

"They'll be shut."

June Gaukroger had encountered the malice of life and things quite often. Just now they seemed personified in Charlie. She uttered certain words but kept them under her breath. She picked up a note pad with gilt pencil attached and scribbled.

"This is a shopping list for the supermarket, fifteen quid's worth of expensive stuff. Give him cash and two baskets, say we are having unexpected guests."

"But it's just around the corner."

"Use your loaf, Charlie. Because of these high buildings it's an expensive market. Even the village idiot would know that if he bussed half a mile to the working class he'd get it for ten per cent less. And once he does that he'll go and get a cup of tea until he works out exactly what he can fiddle you. Say two hours."

"That is smart," said Charlie. "What will you do after?"

"Phone Mum," she said.

Coming out of a Mickey Finn is rather like coming out of an anaesthetic. There is consciousness accompanied by unreality, the mind has no power over the limbs which, however, are capable of movement. Sergeant Reed had the impression that he was somehow dying in a ditch, the limit of his vision being something which looked like a dirty glass plate. He felt his toes wriggle, always a good sign, because if they do not something is seriously wrong. Having collapsed, drunk, in various parts of the British Isles, and once in Flemington, Australia, Reed felt no immediate alarm, but there was a funny taste in his mouth with which he did not immediately associate. He could achieve, drunk, sober or hung over, almost total recall, and he had not really had enough to reduce him to this condition assuming it was not the next day. He squirmed over enough to get a sight of his watch. It was eight.

Then he saw the boots, four pairs of them, around him. His sight was clearing and they were metal-tipped.

"The poor basta'd's bin done," declaimed a voice with built-in adenoids. "Done by the blacks! Don't worry, mister, we'll tory them, we'll show 'em how to get back to Bengal." Reed heard them clicking off in their bovver boots. ·

There was a lamp post and it was an alley, the Sergeant registered. But there was little strength in his legs.

"Are you all right, sir?"

It was a polite Pakistani carrying a monstrously large brief-case.

"Help me up," said Reed. A desire to leak was becoming imperative as his frozen nerves thawed out. With a helping hand and the brace of a brick wall behind him, he struggled to his feet. His overcoat had been replaced, but in such a manner that it was rucked in lumps down his back.

"Where am I?" he asked at length.

"Rosie Street, sir."

Reed shuddered and put the grimy wall to use : you would be considered eccentric if you did not around Rosie Street where the grand old tradition of *gardez-loo* still was practised and occasionally resulted in people being had up in the police court.

"I'm a police officer."

The Pakistani was nervous. "I always get finished before dark. I'm an importer, but today there was the question of new contracts . . ." Fear was making him loquacious.

"They're around with boots on," said Reed, feeling a pain in his chest and back.

"I have a car at the end of the alley, sir."

In an inside pocket of his topcoat the Sergeant found an eight-inch piece of soft lead piping. With numbed fingers he twisted it round the knuckles of his right hand. "Get your keys out and make it fast," he said.

It was on the other side of the alley, shrewdly parked under a powerful street light in Rosie Street itself. Informers lived in a curious symbiosis with the thugs and ponces who had their homes in the street and thus few articles were stolen : minor violence, like kicking brothers from the Great Commonwealth of Nations, was rather different because the police had no funds to reward informers upon this matter unless private property was involved. The Pakistani ran, outstripping Reed, shuffling heavy-footed behind. As the Sergeant emerged from the alley his benefactor was struggling to open the door of the Cortina while clumping, running feet converged.

"Tory 'im. East 'is sewage. Teddy 'im up the pole," hooted the spotty-faced youth who obviously combined the offices of leader and wag. He was leading and Reed hit him in the face.

"What's this?" said another as his bear leader slumped on his knees, bleeding from his nose. The Pakistani was inside the car, reaching back to open the rear door. Reed scrambled in, with the nasty feeling that he might faint.

"Where to, sir?"

Reed considered. The Admiral Byng was roughly two miles away. His wrist watch, with a greasy scum over the glass, registered eight ten. He gave the directions.

Sergeant Jarvis had finally repaired to the Admiral Byng, less from any liking for it than because it was well-warmed and that when he was not home his family were prohibited from turning the gas fire in the living-room to more than half, a general saving which was often substantial in the severer London winters. At five it had been sleeting down as he entered the pub and encountered Mr. Pudding, the Brewery representative, busily engaged upon the English habit of tapping a barometer with a small glass of gin in his free hand. Though Jarvis recoiled, he was prevented by the press of bodies behind him.

Mr. Pudding vaguely recognised the Sergeant. "There's a cold front coming," he greeted as a large lady, fighting her way to the bar, precipitated him against the instrument.

She momentarily glared from under her blue rinse and Jarvis recognised a dignatory of the Australian press. "Mind yer tongue, y' drongo," she snarled without halting her progression.

Pinned next to Mr. Pudding, inhaling a curious compound of expensive scent, imported hair grease, deodorants, and the strong compound of lye with which the Brewery recommended that every inanimate object should be doused, Jarvis said, "Business seems aboom, Mr. P."

"We are buying it in for the Brewery, Mr. Uh, from the

Estate, at a fair price, and installing a manager. The Chairman has a great idea. Encourage the Sunday papers to write articles about the crimes that have been plotted or committed in pubs. Lor' there are thousands of 'em. We might have a discreet bloodstain done in plastic on the floor with the notice that so-and-so was kicked to death here and the like. And the crims themselves—the Chairman is a great one for rehabilitation. Suppose we got some rehabilitated old murderers, quite tame and, say, vouched for by the T.U.C. or something respectable, and put them on display, perhaps with a bit of patriotic patter—'I saw the light when I heard Sir Douglas' sort of thing. People would crowd in, perhaps to see a gory weapon or two in stout glass cases—bless you," Mr. Pudding drained his drop and looked mournfully at the serried buttocks at the bar, "the bastards 'd steal your dentures, let alone the loo seats and toilet paper. We could place a hangman's rope, plastic, o' course, to liven up the liqueur shelves, and the Chairman told us at what we call our Merry Sales Gathering that the guillotine was an English invention designed to keep the working class respectable in northern England in the sixteenth century. We could get a model mocked up, as they say, with no cutting edge and put it in one of the bigger houses. No end to it! Look at that lot at the bar! Luckily I'm a prudent man and laid in a nice little hip flask. But what about you? Nobody could fight through that lot."

"I'll watch," said Sergeant Jarvis, who was looking at some faces with distaste. There was old, cadaverous Dr. Dee prodding his wife viciously in the small of the back to hasten her progress to the bar. A man nearly seven feet tall extended a tweedy arm over the head of a protesting rival for the barmaid's attentions. That would be the man known as Johnny and concealed in the crowd would be his friend, Big Bertie, who was as diminutive as most high-class pickpockets are. The gross man known as Fat had the only deserted place at the bar, a fact attributable to the two 'minders' who flanked him, scarred-face men with greasy-looking hats well pulled down. There were quite a few others, too.

It was strange, thought Jarvis, damned strange. Why should they keep coming back, these people who had seen too much violence to need a vicarious thrill?

A thought struck Jarvis and with a grunt in the direction of Mr. Pudding he sidled along the outside wall until he came to the snack bar, almost deserted at this hour. Tonight there were two young men in white coats serving. Jarvis noticed Joe Pollick wearing, judging by the smell of freshly sized material, a new suit off the peg. He was one of the short-legged men with outsize shoulders who are almost impossible to fit with ready-made coats and trousers.

"The Brewery nipped in ahead of the other bidders and bought the freehold, previously owned by some old lady," said Joe. "Now they've got it lock, bottle and barrel."

Pollick had been drinking, observed Jarvis. "Have an ale and accept congratters."

"I'm not drinking," said Pollick with great gravity. "Anyway I always did prefer the short stuff." His slightly blood-shot eyes caressed the goodies. "What about a nice piece of veal-and-hammer on the Brewery, sir? Lines the stummick. And a whack of the old Commo salad to lubricate the toobs?"

Jarvis accepted and appreciably brightened as he marked 'to supper fifty pence' in his notebook. Pollick, carefully balanced, did the serving himself.

"Tuck into that," he said. "I must go to consult the Brewery Representative."

At the first chew Jarvis realised what had happened. Although rather lethargic when it came to paying suppliers the Brewery on occasions could move with alarming speed—its debt collectors were equipped with motor bikes and walkie-talkies. In taking over the Admiral Byng they had also taken over the food supplies via the huge processing company they had acquired in the process of diversification. Under the new system pie and sausages would consist of healthful vege-table protein and flavourings provided by learned young gents in white coats who had apparently not quite mastered their arcane arts. The mayonnaise on the pale potato salad was innocent of any connection with gnarled and ancient olive trees and would have bemused the eminent soldier who lost a battle and ruined his country while engrossed in its invention. Jarvis remembered in time that so powerful an effect was exercised upon the colon that the wise Brewery had stopped providing toilet paper in the houses it owned in view of the fact that the British public doted on mayonnaise dishes. On the other hand the effect of vegetable protein was directly the reverse so that in combination one was pulled both ways and caught between two stools. The Sergeant, faced with the choice, pushed back the salad and morosely noshed the veal-and-ham pie, its contents a ghastly shade of pink, relieved by chunks of blue hard-boiled egg. The swing doors to the restaurant were bolted. Tomorrow a large kind of steam bath would be installed to accommodate the steel troughs of food which came in from the Hygienic Central Kitchen owned by the Brewery. The sauces and gravies came in the form of white powder in large tins, to be mixed with hot water or reconstituted milk as the case might be. 'As British as Roast Beef', the Brewery described its houses in American travel magazines. Though not a sensitive man, Jarvis could be touched in the stomach and he shuddered as he adhered his massive hindquarters more firmly to the flimsy seat and picked up the *Evening Standard* which somebody had inadvertently put down while going to the loo.

Jarvis was a slow reader who literally read every word from the masthead to the classified ads and even the statutory slug at the bottom of the last page which told you where it was printed. Gradually the crowd grew, eager for vegetable protein doused with sauce. Jarvis read on systematically, oblivious to snarlings, whinings, pushings—you might as well try to push the Rock of Gibraltar—and a large smear of mustard dropped from a hamburger on to the back of his neck. A flatulent spasm as the vegetable protein started to be propelled into his gastric juices finally aroused him in the middle of the stop-press paragraphs. There were nasty looks as he eased to his feet. "My shoes are killing me," said a stout old dowager pointedly as she leapt on to the vacated seat, skirt straining alarmingly.

"But your bum will be warm," muttered Jarvis.

"Poddon!"

"The weather's warm," leered Jarvis, in the direction of the patina of sleet upon the nearest window.

"Man's a cad, Elsie," said a thin, gruff lady with side whiskers and slacks. Or perhaps it was a man, ruminated Jarvis, you couldn't tell these days.

It was a quarter to nine. Jarvis was eminently fair. The Regulations said that after Big Ben boomed nine strokes you could claim sixty pence in 'late money', and Jarvis always religiously stayed on duty until that moment, a fact vouched for by various Home Office accountants who had kept a professional eye upon him. The Sergeant toyed with a gold tooth pick, once the property of an Australian con man who had dropped it when Jarvis, in self-defence it transpired, had hit him in the stomach. The pub was still crowded, but the crowd, as crowds do, had got itself roughly organised; so he was able to make his way into the saloon bar without too much difficulty. Every chair and table was occupied. His bedizened, mottled nose glowing, Mr. Pudding was starting a Brewery day book in the cubicle once occupied by Harry Alwyn. You had to pay them, the Brewery Auditors, mused Jarvis, up to every kind of trick to pinch a public penny in a legal way. Old Dr. Dee and his wife had departed, he noted, but Johnny and Big Bertie were drinking tumblers of crème de menthe and lemonade.

Hello! said Jarvis to himself. There was old Mrs. Stoney, undeterred by previous police visitations. And with her, Jarvis waited for the profile, was Mrs. Gaukroger, wearing a purple pyjama suit under her Persian lamb coat. Mrs. Stoney, in between sips of gin-and-tonic, was glancing at the far end of the bar. It took Jarvis, with all his experience, some time to get it in focus. Mrs. Stoney's leers and meaningful glances were directed at a certain Mr. Tupper who, being a strict teetotaller and the purveyor of humorous monologues at church gatherings, was drinking the acidulous brew of sparkling grapefruit which the Brewery produced as a by-product of one of its subsidiary factories engaged in making patent expectorant cough mixture. A tallish, thin, bald man, Mr. Tupper was virtually invisible, the perfect man in the street, with the proviso that Mr. Tupper was on occasions off the street and in gaol. Jarvis gloomily wondered how he squared it with his church activities, though Superintendent Quant had once opined at a staff meeting that there must be a lot of good in the chap if one dug down deep enough, which was apposite in a way because Mr. Tupper— nobody referred to him by his Christian name—was a Searcher, a highly paid underworld vocation. In view of the fact that today no safe or vault was unsmashable, householders and companies were dreaming up hiding places. Jarvis knew one diamond merchant who kept his parcels inside a fake cistern in the ladies' loo. As Marx might have foretold, the result was a breed of men like Mr. Tupper who ferreted out valuables as a hog will truffles. Get Mr. Tupper into a building—and he was afraid of heights and not agile —and he infallibly spotted fake partitions, hidden cavities in concrete floors and once, according to Records, a diamond tiara which a Dowager Duchess, appalled by the insurance premiums, had caused to be baked inside a Christmas cake. To be fair, it was believed that his sweet tooth, often possessed by the unco' godly, had led Mr. Tupper to it, but nevertheless it had been fenced in Belgium for seventeen thousand pounds and now, unrecognisably remodelled, adorned the bosom of the wife of a prosperous horse-meat dealer. He was considered by the Underworld as a kind of super witch-doctor, though his rheumatic knees, made worse by their constant contact with the floors of dank chapels, hindered the getaway considerably. Four times Mr. Tupper had been abandoned to the wolves of the law by his companions, and although on the first the exhortations of a fatherly pastor had caused the judge to release him he had subsequently served a total of eight years inside. On his next conviction he would be sentenced as a 'habitual' so now he got into the premises on some pretext and passed on the information gained by his large cowlike eyes to those who did the actual smashing. A man of principle, he refused to have anything to do with the theft of ecclesiastical property of Christian origin, even if Roman Catholic. In a good year he made five thousand pounds tax free and gave a tenth to charity.

As these thoughts passed through his head Jarvis noted that Mrs. Stoney was being much less than discreet in the manner in which she repeatedly tried to catch Mr. Tupper's placid eyes and direct them towards the various cupboards and receptacles around the bar. Once Mr. Tupper, caught by her beady gaze, wagged his bald head in a sign of reproach. The old lady must have had recourse to the bottle, decided Jarvis, while her daughter, immaculately groomed and beautiful, was decidedly hung over. Joe Pollick was pouring her a Fernet Branca.

Jarvis thought he might call for reinforcements, for Mr. Tupper's presence never presaged anything good. At worst he could spin it out until midnight with the snug allowances he could claim after that hour. He ordered synthetic orange squash, keeping his back to the ladies and aided by the fact he had had no personal dealings with Mr. Tupper. He felt somebody come to the bar on his right side and had to venture a sly side glance. It was Reed and Jarvis had never seen him look worse, even in the old days when he did a stint with the licensing squad and spent his time trying to buy spirits out of permitted hours; but that had been years ago and tonight the Sergeant looked old and battered as he stood there applying a red spotted handkerchief to a running nose.

"Tupper's here," Jarvis muttered.

"It's a hellishing nasty night out," growled Reed whose every vertebra ached. He was looking malevolently at Mrs.

Gaukroger. Nothing he could do there, though. Drinking on duty, half slopped in somebody's living-room—a half-good defence counsel could have got Jack the Ripper off, with a donation out of the Poor Box, if equipped with such ammunition. He would have to grin and bear it. During his journey with the Pakistani he had cudgelled his brains to no avail, but he was a man who hated to be beaten and he placed Mrs. Gaukroger in his mental pending file alongside a lot of other people who would have been alarmed had they known. At the moment he contented himself with giving the lady a glance which would surely have curdled her blood had she not been protected against a cruel world by a patina of gin.

Jarvis noticed the glance because it was unlike Reed with his deceptive placidity to reveal his feelings in such a manner. And his colleague invariably dressed neatly and expensively. There was a touch of green envy to Jarvis's thoughts: it was widely supposed that he outfitted himself at the Lost Property Office sales although it was in fact at a second-hand dealer in a grim Soho Alley where the goods were improbably labelled 'from a gentleman's wardrobe'. He noticed that Reed's topcoat was steaming damp and his shoes saturated, while the collar of his silk shirt had black grease upon it. He was hatless, too.

"Look as though you crawled out of a bush!" commented Jarvis.

"I said it was filthy outside. A man should be at home with his family."

"You couldn't speak truer," intoned Jarvis hypocritically. Perhaps it was the sight of Reed's nose, like a mauve strawberry, surmounting his sodden garments, but in spite of the general over-heating—'Above all keep them warm,' the benevolent Chairman of the Brewery was wont to instruct his neophytes, 'warm beer on a sweaty August night they'll lap up but cold, my dear sirs, drives them home immediately' —Jarvis seemed to apprehend a distinct drop in the room temperature. He felt a twinge of alarm because though he was almost certain that he could spot the unauthorised excessive use of his family gas fire, he was not sure in these permissive days that his four children had not found a way to fiddle it, and of course their mother always sided with the kids.

"Place is rife with villains," he said.

"I saw Mrs. Gaukroger at her flat," said Reed, straightening his aching torso, for it was important to him to get his story on record. "She told me a lot of cock-and-bull about her family history and Gaukroger, her husband, but nothing we did not already know."

"The old woman has plenty of brains," Jarvis replied, eyeing her openly, "and so her daughter probably has some. A smart piece of goods!" His tone was disapproving as he could never see a pretty woman without lust competing with the computed cost of dressing her. He altered the subject. "Mr. Tupper's on my left and the old bitch keeps ogling and signalling to him."

"Old Tup!" Thrice had Reed pulled in the sanctimonious man and listened to him extol the virtues of total temperance in the back seat of the police car. He swiftly turned his head. "Where?"

"Gone!" groaned Jarvis. "Slipped away while we were gasbagging. I might have known." Mr. Tupper was renowned for his talent of fading gently from the scene. "I tell you, Mr. Reed, that we need reinforcements. Dr. Dee was in here, and others I noticed were Fat and his minders, plus Johnny and his little pickpocketing pard. Plus quite a few others." He had plonked it well and truly into Reed's corner, the senior man having to make the decision.

Reed remembered that there was a call box a hundred yards away. He nodded, groaned, put down his quarter-full tankard, belched and made his way into the sleety coldness, fumbling in his pocket for change. He had to wait ten minutes while a young citizen of revolting health and good cheer quacked into the handset. But he finally got through to Quant who so loved late hours that he rarely left the Yard before midnight.

It so happened that the Superintendent was impaled upon the problem of transvestism, a report being urgently needed at the Home Office, more and more Englishmen adopting a cult of skirts and ladies' combinations. There was trouble in the factories between rival factions, and at least one with-it Member of Parliament had been rebuked by the Speaker for wearing a green pyjama suit. To their surprise the eminent jurists employed by the Crown had discovered there was no law against it. A snide remark about Britannia had been made by the French President, disappointed that the lady would not totally support the French farming industry, and the whole matter had landed upon the ageing Super's desk. In his thorough way, Quant had sent out for a pair of ladies' combinations, employing Sergeant Humphrey for the task. He was staring at them reflectively, wondering if it would aid his thoughts if he donned them, when Reed came through.

"We had the place gone through thoroughly," mused Quant, "though like all the old licensed houses it is, underneath the tarting up, a dirty old warren of a place. There was nothing and our best men did the job. But obviously Dr. Dee, etcetera, think that there is something hidden. I wonder if Mr. Tupper spotted anything, a cavity under a sink now, they have a considerable number of them on large licensed premises and the late Harry Alwyn, when painted in, appears a rather subtle man. I have got great faith in Mr. Tupper : it's a great pity he has a mote among his moral principles. I'll send two men in plain clothes along *pronto* and don't forget to keep an eye on Mr. Tupper."

"We lost him!"

"What's that?"

"One minute he was there, the next he wasn't."

Quant gave his rusty chuckle. "That sounds like Mr. Tupper. Look in the most unlikely places. I remember that once he found a secret compartment in the bottom of a dustbin and again he spotted that Hindu with heroin inside a glass eye : Big Bertie stole it off his bedside table. Ah well, I'm a busy man this night. Goodbye."

While he looked at a list of available staff, the old Superintendent had a startling and disturbing thought about ladies' combs. Could you impregnate them with heroin in solution, wash them later and reconstitute the drug? Even the most choleric Customs inspectress would not actually wash garments. There was a lot of sin around. He would get on to the Customs on the morrow.

The two men Quant dispatched by cab were not cheerful in any way for they had looked forward to a cosy evening of cocoa and solo with some of the other boys in the pool. Nothing generally happened until the early hours of the morning which required C.I.D. presence and then it was almost time to knock off. Instead they had to go into the freezing streets.

"Jarvis is there," groaned one, "talking about his goddamned rheumatics to any old harpy who'll listen and swizzing sparkling fruit juice on the side."

"There's Reed," said his mate. "He's always good for a short one and a meat pie. A gentleman."

"But then you have to carry him home! I don't know how he gets away with it."

"Influence," proclaimed the younger constable, incorrectly, "there ain't no justice on our side of the counter."

"Too right!" His senior tweaked his freezing nose, preparatory to paying off the morose taxi driver.

The Admiral Byng had closed its delights. Inflated by Brewery beer and made dyspeptic by synthetic pie, elderly people were waiting for non-existent cabs. There was an unseemly scramble as the two constables alighted.

"I was here first."

"You certainly were not!"

"Piss off, all of youse," said the driver with great satisfaction, " 'cause I'm knocking off for the night. You

boorjuice don't expect a worker to close 'is bleedin' eyes."
With a snarl of gears he drove into the freezing night.

Faced with naked revolt and the distant rumbles of tumbrils, the bourgeoisie closed its frightful ranks.

"Get his number, Flo!" commanded a palpable Old Etonian.

"But I haven't a pen, Alec."

"The police, call them at once!" commanded a vast dowager from the depths of her musquash.

"Alfred, dolling, I simply must have a loo. This cold is nipping me."

"Get along quick," instructed the senior constable. They tapped discreetly on the pub door. No answer! Behind them howlings at imaginary taxis proliferated. They banged and kicked.

"What's this?" Welcome, healing, hot fug enveloped them as Joe Pollick half opened the door, one foot jammed behind it. Over his shoulder the great, inflamed face of Mr. Pudding eyed the freezing outside world with disfavour.

"Police reinforcements for Sergeant Reed."

"Half shot!" said Pollick, "and his mate cleaning up a broken bag of potato crisps. Come on in."

"I say!" It was a moon-faced man in a waterproofed tweed coat and bowler hat, followed by a diminutive blonde. "We must have the ladies' toilet."

"A Brewery Toilet," wheezed Mr. Pudding, aghast, "after licensing hours! People must control themselves, sir, like the Brewery. If Mr. Heath, God bless him, should make a requeshst like that, I should refer him to Constitutional Law and he would obey the lawsh of his country." Somewhat overcome, Mr. Pudding walked rapidly backwards, listing slightly.

"It's the cold, it's nipped her," whined the moon-faced man.

Inevitably, a few members of the gentry had become interested onlookers, thus forming the nucleus of a crowd. Glancing behind him the senior constable grimaced. This was the sort of scene which could leave an indelible dirty mark upon a record sheet. Years would erase circumstances leaving only the faded inscription, 'cannot control the public'. No promotion for a man like that!

"All right, landlord," he said, "let these two people in to briefly use the amenities of the house."

"Gennelmen." The night air percolating in was too much for Mr. Pudding who was weaving back. "Gennelmen, a short one on the Brewery to shelebrate."

"I do not appreciate your tone," snapped the moon-faced man, but Mr. Pudding had made a corpulent turn and was leading the way to the saloon bar. The blonde lady speeded her steps and vanished.

Over and above its warmth and the smell of people and beer, there was a stale atmosphere and a general look of tawdriness, as is seen in a theatre being aired out in the morning. Reed, both hands on the bar top, stared impassively at a whisky calendar featuring a red-coated huntsman. Jarvis was tipping shards of potato crisps into one palm.

"Put out the rum, Joe," commanded Mr. Pudding, making one of his successful landings on the shores of sobriety.

"Well, I don't mind if I do," said the moon-faced man, placated, "but none for the missus on account of her weakness, I'm sure."

Reed's lack-lustre eyes swivelled sideways at the bottle as Joe Pollick poured six measures.

"And a drop of peppermint, Joe," said the Sergeant, "but don't drown it."

The blonde lady came clacking back. "There's a man in the ladies' doing things to a cistern."

"Wot's he doing of to a Brewery Cistern?" demanded Pudding, outraged speculation spreading over his face.

The lady was indignant. "How do I know what he was doing to the bloody cistern? He must have been standing on the seat, the dirty beast. I saw him in the gap over the door of one of the cubicles." She had all the confidence and aggression of a relieved bladder.

"What kind of man?" asked Jarvis, brushing chip-dust off his coat.

"It's disgraceful and disgusting!"

"Did you go, love?" bleated the moon-faced man and sustained a contemptuous glance.

"Come along, Alfred!" she commanded. Resignedly Joe Pollick followed them to the door.

Reed and Mr. Pudding were gazing into their glasses like gypsies at a crystal ball. Jarvis groaned to the two constables, "Arrest the loiterer in the ladies'!"

"What charge, Mr. Jarvis?" asked the elder stolidly.

"On premises outside hours," said Jarvis at length.

He watched them unenthusiastically depart. "I can smell trouble," he told Reed. But there was no trouble. The constables returned, each with a hand upon a nondescript man, a mousy-haired, bloodless-faced individual, whose very lips and eyes defied description. His name was Piper.

With a visible effort Reed asserted himself. "Explain yourself!"

In a totally colourless voice the man said, "My eyesight's bad, gentlemen, something terrible, and the glasses got smashed when my nipper trod on them. You know how long you have to wait..."

"I don't give a damn," said Reed, recognising that Jarvis might be drawn into a lengthy discussion about opticians. Once you perfected a line of patter such as Jarvis had it became a habit. "Who are you?"

A flaccid tongue tip momentarily appeared. "Tommy Piper, sir, living in the Borough and unemployed. I was told there might be a watchman's job in the vicinity."

"So you applied for it in the ladies'!" said Reed.

"Half a mo'," said the junior constable. "Tommy Piper! There's a fellow of that name just come back on the street after doing two for breaking and entering a supermarket."

"They had a concealed camera, sir. Now *that's* not playing the game."

"Piper," said Reed thoughtfully. "Don't you fence through Dr. Dee?"

"The good Doctor has been a wonderful friend to me," said Piper. "He tries to get me honest employment." He looked as sanctimonious as his features allowed.

"What were you doing mucking around with the cistern?" Reed thrust his face within inches of the nondescript man's face.

"He wasn't at it when we got him," said the senior constable. "He was knocking at the door."

"It had jammed," said Piper, "and I was trying to get out like. The lady saw me trying to get over the top of the door."

The junior constable sighed. "In the execution of my duty I trod on the seat, slightly cracking it and fished in the cistern."

"Property of the Brewery!" moaned Mr. Pudding.

From his overcoat pocket, the constable fished a small plastic bag and laid it on the counter. There was a piece of celluloid, a few keys and a collection of tiny metal tools. "It was on the floor."

"Never seen it in my born days," declaimed Piper without looking.

And, of course, you couldn't prove it, was the thought in all their heads, but Reed, from habit, went into the usual act. "There are two ways we can play this, Piper, and one of them's sweet!"

"Hundreds of people each day use the carsies in a pub, guv, what with the quality of the beer and the meat pies. Hundreds."

"Do you mean ladies carry housebreaking tools in their handbags?" The Sergeant inadvertently brought his weight down on Piper's instep.

"Now, guv," whined the little thief, "no offence meant or taken I'm sure."

"I've a good mind to take you outside," said Reed.

"Excuse me, Sergeants all." It was Joe Pollick catfooting

back. "But there's a funny noise in the off-licence storeroom. I hadn't locked it, though I have now."

"Did you look inside?"

"Not likely, a little fellow like me!"

"You stay here," Reed admonished Piper. "The rest of us will take a look."

Joe Pollick meditatively took up an empty beer bottle.

The bottle department was an extension of the public bar noteworthy for the fact that it had escaped the day's dirt and grime which covered the bar floors. The storeroom had a neat green-painted door with a large lock.

Reed unlocked it and whipped it open, freezing momentarily as Johnny towered over him from the inside, but the pleasant baritone voice said quickly, "It's only me and my dear boy, Sergeant, who have got locked in after mistaking it for the front door." Big Bertie trotted out behind him.

Reed sighed, but was still wary as Johnny was on the 'suspected killer' file in connection with the still unexplained death of a car thief who had been strangled.

"Search 'em!" The elder constable ran experienced hands over them. Big Bertie giggled, was quelled by Johnny's ferocious scowl. The constable shrugged after ten minutes.

"Nothing, sir, but a bit of 'loid in Bertie's pocket."

"The dear boy uses it to measure cloth. He makes his own things," said Johnny glibly.

The younger constable said something, but Jarvis swiftly stepped in front of Johnny.

"Look here," said Reed. "Whether there will be a charge I do not know, but if you try to scarper I'll throw the book at you. Still living at 'Appy 'Ampstead?"

"Yes," said Johnny, "and we won't go out tomorrow. I'm making my veal bolognese."

"Oh Johnny!" said Big Bertie in minor ecstasy.

"Put them out the door and lock it after them," said Reed to the constables and watched them go.

"I don't know what my Chairman will say," said Mr. Pudding, who had watched from a discreet distance.

"He had better keep his bloody mouth shut," said Reed, "because licences can be revoked on police objection."

Mr. Pudding's face became more purple. "Do you know what the Brewery gives to party funds? My dear sir, they come to *see* the Chairman. Rolls-Royce he did not like, his own having gearbox trouble which vexed him, but the wool industry he might save."

Once again Reed thought that here might be a comfortable lurk for semi-retirement. "We'd better take a general look round," he said.

Piper was waiting like a chained sheep. "Did you get them, guv?"

"Shaddup," said Reed, rubbing his nose and taking off his overcoat. He was nearly dry in more ways than one, but for once Mr. Pudding, full of thoughts concerning Brewery Property, did not come to the party.

"We won't get anything out of Johnny," Reed told Jarvis. "You could beat him to pulp and he wouldn't talk."

"Big Bertie?" asked one of the constables.

"A gutsy little bloke, and besides dead scared of his master. Any old how it's not Johnny's type of crime. He's a revengeful character who broods, but he doesn't bash over the head on the spur of the moment. Besides which there is no talk of him falling out with Harry Alwyn."

"I tell you, guv, and give me credit for it before the Beak," said Piper with a shade of colour to his voice, "that Johnny liked Harry Alwyn. You must know that most of Johnny's loot goes out of the country and Harry was always fair to him. And you know what?"

"How the devil should I know what."

"In the corner, guv," wheedled Piper. Reed found he had fearsome breath and like all with this misfortune apparently delighted to broadcast the fact.

"I'd rather not be charged, guv," said Piper in the corner, "on account of me courting a widow with a nice annuity. She's dead ugly but with thirty-seven nicker a week before tax."

"It could be arranged," said Reed.

"You're a gentleman," said Piper without noticeable fervour, "and I trust you like I would my old father. Johnny and Big Bertie were doing a job in Bedchester, Dorset, on the night that Harry had his skull fixed. A coupla thousand quid in diamonds, like, but I dunno where they stashed it. Rare sly, they are."

"And the old Doctor?"

"Fair's fair, guv. The good old Doc ain't a man to fiddle with as you know."

"All right," said Reed. "I'll let you out the front door myself but Christ help you next time I see you."

"Upstairs?" Joe Pollick said. "Well I locked the door to the staircase and here's the keys. And I'm going home, Mr. Pudding, the hours being long enough as they are, and overtime not bein' conspicuous in the agreement I signed."

"A willing worker never thinks of hours," declaimed Mr. Pudding.

"This one likes his bleedin' kip," said Pollick, bouncing the keys on the bar top, "so have somebody here at eight ack emma to let me in. The place is filthy and I told old Mrs. Crippen to bring her daft sister-in-law to lend a hand. Well, I'm off."

Reed locked the door behind him and returned to the bar where Mr. Pudding had lapsed into a kind of bemused silence.

Beckoning Jarvis and the two constables, Reed led the way to the snack bar. Outside the dining-room doors, still firmly locked as he tested them, was one leading to the stairs.

"Unlocked!" he said as he twisted the handle.

Jarvis dug in his hip pocket and produced a set of brass knuckles. The constables had eight-inch truncheons and Reed dug out his useful bit of lead piping. The door opened outwards and in spite of its refurbishing the smell of old buildings crept down the stairs. Professionally, the senior constable kept behind the door, his mate a convenient six feet away. They listened, but the only sound was the distant, stertorous wheezing of Mr. Pudding who was talking to himself about the Brewery and its wisdom.

Creaky and painful at the knees, Reed led the way up. As in all pub buildings of its period, the staircase lacked banisters and the risers were narrow and precipitous, emitting mouse-like squeakings from under the carpeting. To the right of the narrow landing was the late Harry Alwyn's one-roomed flat which, under the prurient licensing laws, should be locked at all times to protect the bed against onslaughts of the peasantry inflamed by libations of the Brewery Ale. It was, alas, open and Reed, cautiously peeking, espied a couple seated on the bed.

"Gawd," he said wearily. "It's Georgie Thigh and his girl friend Thelma. I suppose you thought it was the front door?"

"It was passion that brought us up here, Mr. Reed," said saucy Thelma.

"And you and Georgie living for six years at Streatham! Two kids now, aren't there?"

"Who knows the depths of the human heart?" asked Thelma.

"I suppose you don't know anything about these?" asked the senior constable, bending to pick up a small bunch of keys and a file off the floor.

"Never seen them in our lives, sir," retorted Thelma, and her *de facto* snickered.

The policemen looked at the keys balanced on a broad palm. Reed said, "We might see what a jury thinks."

"You honestly would not get a committal," said Georgie Thigh.

The police, although his natural enemies, did not dislike Georgie, a technical school drop-out who had found, aged eighteen, that he preferred stealing cars to sinking into the warm embraces of the Welfare State. He was in no way violent and supported in part a home for aged donkeys, although nearly all criminals like animals and are liked by them. Thelma, thought Reed, was the smarter of the two. At the age of thirteen she had thought up the dodge of stealing the uniform of a famous school for females of the aristocracy. In this she purchased first-class tickets in railway trains going to Liverpool, shrewd beyond her years on two counts. A lesser brain would have saved on the ticket and also not realised that Liverpool business men are noted for satyriasis. At a certain stage young Thelma would seize the communication cord and demand twenty pounds. Innocent or not her fellow traveller paid. Whatever they did, there were at least two Sunday papers that would pay Thelma handsomely for her story, a fact she did not omit to point out. They got her at last when she importuned a bishop in mufti—he was secretly negotiating to become a Mormon missionary at a higher salary—but it took a long time and entailed periscopes, listening devices, and the near apoplexy of a stout female sergeant who used to lie under railway seats in high summer. Being sixteen, Thelma got bound over and put into a home for fallen girls. A crusading lawyer made his reputation by establishing the fact, via eminent surgeons, that Thelma was not technically fallen and she went to London and a life of genteel prostitution. At eighteen she met Georgie Thigh. Reed knew her to be a witty, capable young lady interested in Indonesian cooking, who would eventually flog her memoirs.

"You can search me," offered Georgie.

"And me, sir," said Thelma with a send-up leer at Jarvis, who sniffed in disapproval.

"Off the record, Georgie, what were you after?"

"General pickin's. Harry handled a welter of stuff, and what might be lying about is fair game. If you got it it would be unidentifiable, medium-carat stuff from all ends of Europe; so it would go into Consolidated Revenue to support germ-warfare factories. It might as well buy me and Thelly a year hogging it in Bermuda."

They could always rationalise it, thought Reed. He said, "How straight was Harry?"

Thigh was no fool. "In our game honesty is often the best policy among ourselves. If you knew the ropes Harry would give you a fair price. Cash and no trouble. O' course he never handled the really big stuff, except . . ." He hesitated.

"The bank-robbery loot?"

"So the scuttle-butt said, but that is out of my class as you well know."

"Did you know that he was ringing in counterfeit for the real stuff and selling it several times over?"

Georgie looked diffident and Thelma gave him a shut-up look.

"I did hear a whisper," said Georgie after an over-long silence. "It's a trick what has been done before, but it's dangerous. The old Doctor was worried about his cash, so the whisper went, and Dee is not the man you want to be worrying. When it's the Big Money, Mr. Reed, you have to be right careful . . ."

"And so you better cease nattering," said Thelma. "What is the charge, officers and gents, in this permissive society?"

"Go quiet as lambs and let a police matron search you."

"Me, but not Georgie. Him I do not trust with matrons."

"Mr. Higgins," Reed addressed the elder constable, "you will telephone for a police car and take these two people in on suspish. If they are clean there will be no immediate charge."

"Christ! You look hung over!" said Thelma. "What about drinks all round?"

Reed wished she were dead. "Lock the doors behind them," he told Jarvis, "and push Mr. Pudding out with them." All that grog lying fallow and untouchable below.

"As a tip," said Thelma, cryptically, "you might look in the bathroom whence comes furtive noises. Or did."

"Thelly!" said Georgie.

"Dog eats dog," she said, powdering her small nose, "especially an old bitch like Mr. Tupper. He called me a scarlet woman once and I've never liked the colour."

"Take them down, please."

139

"Mr. Tupper won't run for it," he told the younger constable later, "because his gams are weak and his knees something awful on account of all that praying bringing on rheumatics. He's a nice old cock, very greedy on sweets and pastry. Wait on the landing in case there is a reversal of form."

"I know Mr. Tupper," said the constable. "Ever seen his wife?"

"No," said Reed, momentarily fascinated.

"Gawd!"

Gingerly the Sergeant tested the bathroom door. It was bolted within.

"If I have to break this door down, Mr. Tupper," Reed roared, "you'll bloody well regret it."

There were curious noises within the bathroom. What on earth could Mr. Tupper be doing?

"Excuse me, I'm sure," answered a reedy tenor, "but I was caught short and the catch jammed."

"I'll catch you by the short hairs!" Reed was provoked beyond all measure. Nevertheless he had to wait until Jarvis returned. "The old bastard's in there and he won't come out."

"You feel that way after Brewery pie," whined Jarvis, who was looking pale. He raised his voice. "Did you have the veal-and-ham, Mr. Tupper?"

"A portion, sir," returned Mr. Tupper, "and the deep-frozen gooseberry, which triggered me off. Talk of those bombs, sir, they are nothing to the Brewery pies."

There were noises of something being moved. Like the sound of wheels, thought Reed. "Mr. Tupper, open or I'll break through and Christ help you!"

"Just this minute, sir. Just this minute." There were shuffling sounds and the door opened. Mr. Tupper respectfully doffed his hat as Jarvis pushed roughly past him.

"Can't you wait?" snarled Reed, cessation of drink making him feel queasy himself.

"There are times which wait for no man," said Jarvis,

putting on his bowler to protect himself from the icy draught from the small louvred window.

"I must say," said the constable, a stalwart of the Police Association, "that a man can hardly be expected to work in such conditions."

"Have you ever taken a corpse out of the river at low tide?" asked Reed. "We have to work in all conditions and not consider our feelings."

"But a corpse can't help itself," said the constable doggedly.

"Personal remarks about a senior officer are subject to a disciplinary board," groaned Jarvis.

"I'll be a witness, Mr. Reed," volunteered Mr. Tupper. "Aren't your bowels filled with compassion?" he upbraided the constable.

"Well, I doubt it; not having eaten since midday although being entitled to, I'm not full of anything."

Life was getting a bit beyond Reed. Lately he found it did during the winter months. In summer, with London notoriously two degrees higher than the rest of the country both temperature and smell wise, he luxuriated in the hot concrete canyons, but in winter came discontent and rheumatics. He sat down heavily on the edge of the bath and felt movement. By chance his eyes were fixed on Mr. Tupper's and he saw some kind of flicker. The Sergeant arose and examined the bath.

"Mind me!" grumbled Jarvis, his overcoat swathed around him.

There was something odd about the set-up. The two taps were not fixed to the bath itself, but protruded from the wall above. Bending with difficulty, Reed peered down the plug hole. It appeared to empty into some gully trap underneath instead of conventional piping. He grabbed and pulled.

"Mind my bleeding feet!" exclaimed Jarvis as the bath rolled out on concealed castors.

Reed steadied it and looked at Mr. Tupper. "Just show

141

me where it is," he said, "and you'll be in the clear. Any evasion and you'll see how nasty I can get."

"Out a little bit more, sir," said Mr. Tupper, producing a penknife and looking at the plastic tiles. He sidled round, bent and probed. There was a click and a section two feet square sprang up.

"They are much in favour now, sir, though obvious. I checked the toilet and the medicine cupboard and they are clean. These days I find you look at the bath first, though kitchen stoves with false backs are all the rage with the drug traffickers."

Tupper was talking too much which meant nervousness. Reed peered into the cavity. It only contained a bottle a quarter filled with green Chartreuse. There was a patina of black blood and hair on one side. It popped into his mind that the inventors of the stuff had said that nature ordained seven hours sleep, fashion dictated eight, and sin demanded ten. But Harry Alwyn was going to rest for a very long time.

"You saw it?" he asked Tupper.

"Yes, dreadful, but there is a great deal of wickedness in every parish these days, sir."

"Any idea who did it?"

"Alwyn always had a smile," commented Tupper lugubriously, "and such men are not to be trusted. He liked profane jokes, God rest his soul."

"It's the murder weapon, a bottle of green Chartreuse," Reed told Jarvis who was mobile again.

"Argh!" said Jarvis, weakly.

Reed rather shared his feelings. It was a long step home. His wife, with the Viennese chocolates she doted on, would long since have retired to bed flanked by her handy rack of the works of Georgette Heyer. Up here there was comfortable central heating in Harry Alwyn's flat.

"See that Mr. Tupper's clean," he told the constable, but Mr. Tupper had already put on his hat and was divesting himself of overcoat and jacket. There was nothing except a purse with five pounds in it and three temperance tracts in the hip pocket. The Sergeant himself had a go, reasoning that if Mr. Tupper was a whiz at finding things he was probably ditto at concealing them. Of course, if there were diamonds Mr. Tupper would have swallowed them, but investigation entailed a fluoroscope and Reed did not feel up to organising it and the constable was mumbling and becoming mutinous. It was oppressive, too.

"Mr. Jarvis," he said, "these premises should be guarded tonight. I doubt whether reinforcements can be got."

"And count me out," said the constable, "or the Association will take it up."

Jarvis was never slow on the uptake. It was up to four pounds fifty new pence a night plus liberal breakfast allowance and sundries.

"I'll volunteer," he said, "if I can phone the missus."

"They shouldn't send officers out who can't master their bowels," said the constable in the direction of the ceiling.

"Render to Caesar what is Caesar's," said Mr. Tupper.

"Look here," said Reed, "Mr. Jarvis and I will make ourselves as comfortable as best we may in the line of duty. You and Mr. Tupper can go."

"And I suppose we walk the freezin' streets and me with a hole in one sole."

"You can hop for all I care, but I'll authorise the use of a cab."

Reed watched them go down the stairs, Mr. Tupper pitpattering in the lead, fluorescent light gleaming on his white bald head. He guessed his colleague would be telephoning Mrs. Jarvis to impress upon her that there was no need to use both sides of the electric blanket and that half the morning coffee essence was all that was needed. He badly wanted a drink. He pushed away the thought of pillaging the stock downstairs as too dangerous. Drunk or sober Mr. Pudding missed little and Jarvis was capable of bearing witness. A thought struck him and he went back to the bathroom. Taking his handkerchief he pulled out the bottle of green Chartreuse and slowly drank exactly half the remaining liquid. It was like fire in his belly and quite suddenly he realised he was drunk. He walked portentously into Alwyn's flat relishing its snugness. Taking off clothes until he was left with shirt, trousers, socks and shoes he collapsed on the bed and passed out.

He might have known it, gloomed Jarvis, twenty minutes later—the line had been engaged, his wife having been gassing interminably to her old mother who couldn't sleep in cold weather. Reed, drunk or sober, always got the best of things. There was a large easy chair in the corner which he had to make do with, but as he stripped down to rather unpleasantly baggy combinations he realised that the wind had crept around his heart and he would have to sit there listening to Reed's honking breathing.

CHAPTER SIX

Jarvis possessed a watch filched from Unclaimed Lost Property. Invented by a Swiss maniac it possessed a powerful alarm which often went off at the wrong moment, but that morning it started its jangle at seven five.

"Wozzermazzer?" exclaimed Reed, sitting up, momentarily bemused.

"You've died and gone to heaven," said Jarvis, sourly, climbing into worn blue serge trousers. "I'm God and have first right to the bathroom."

Reed was not disposed to doubt him and spent a quarter of an hour staring at his shoes and massaging one aching temple until Jarvis returned in stockinged feet.

"There's an electric razor in the medicine cupboard," he observed. "And water's hot."

Reed shaved, not very successfully, dabbled around his face and drank three glassfuls of heavily chlorinated water. He felt like sitting down and realised that he had not eaten for nearly twenty-four hours. Somewhere in his overcoat pockets was a chocolate bar, but he recoiled at the thought.

Going back to Jarvis he asked piteously, "Any chance of some grub, say a bit of bacon?"

"I feel that way," said Jarvis, "acute dyspepsia—acquired in the line of duty—producing hunger, so I find, but, Lord love us, I won't tackle Brewery food any more."

Eventually, it was Jarvis who found two stale rolls and an opened tin of condensed milk which they ate in melancholy fashion until Joe Pollick knocked thunderously at the door.

The new manager, his official suit already looking rather the worse for wear, was flanked by Mrs. Crippen, wearing what was apparently an ancient ski suit, and her daft relative, talking quietly to herself, and behind him, looking exactly as he had at midnight, was Mr. Pudding and an outsize Gladstone bag.

"Up betimes," said the Brewery auditor, "owing to the fact that my Chairman, who rarely sleeps, phoned me."

"I should tell you, sir," said Reed as they gathered in the saloon bar, "that we apprehended several trespassers on the premises and Mr. Jarvis and I remained on duty all night."

"Remarkable," Mr. Pudding squinted his little eyes. "Joe, mix Sergeant Reed a Fernet Branca and lemonade and take a quick look at the stock."

Jarvis bridled, but Reed drank the concoction with gratitude.

"Tell me, sir," said Pudding, all business, "what does it cost to hire a police officer?"

"Five pounds *per diem* for a constable, fifteen for an Inspector, but always provided it is in the public interest."

"My guv'nor is so delighted with the returns that he wants immediate action to sustain public interest, to wit a uniformed constable spying on a crook who should have scars and a broken nose together with little ferrety eyes. The constable should keep poking his head round a partition sizing him up."

"You wouldn't be able to hire a man for that," said Jarvis firmly.

"Then we'll have to settle for two wrong 'uns giving each other evil glances. My guv is getting on to the Prisoners' Aid people, who the Brewery contributes right handsomely to, old lags being good customers when on the street, but that means tomorrow and he wants action *now*. Surely there must be some obvious crooks around."

"Never heard of any," said Joe Pollick without enthusiasm.

"Only the merchant bankers and they don't looked crooked until they get in the dock," said Jarvis, who had done badly in unit trusts.

"There was a fellow in our street wot they got last year for indigent exposure," piped Mrs. Crippen, who had been following the conversation with interest.

"Would he impress the ladies?" wondered Mr. Pudding aloud.

"Dunno, sir, I was at 'ome. 'E was in a shop doorway in the dark but the P.C., a rare nosy bastid, parm my French, flashed 'is torch and seen it. A little fellow 'e is wiv a outsize 'ead."

"Not suitable," said Pudding, "my guv'nor not wishing sex to rear its head on Brewery property so to speak. Can't you suggest anything? Joe, give Mr. Reed a lubricant drop of brandy."

The Sergeant was too far gone to resent being patronised and Pollick poured for him from the best bottle. It helped considerably. A thought occurred to him. "Try a theatrical agency. Times are always tough among actors, and a good pro can look more like a crook than a crook can, if you follow me, and on stage detectives look a bloody sight more like detectives..." As usual when at the acute hangover stage, Reed felt himself drifting away on knobbly clouds of verbiage. He called a halt, but Mr. Pudding was leering and wagging his head with pleasure. "The very thing," he said. "To work Pudding, to work in the Brewery interests! And you ladies, we want this looking like a new pin because the Chairman is sure to put his head round the door and he misses nothing. Nothing!"

Mr. Pudding scuttled to his cubicle and the telephone, and Reed and Jarvis went out the front door to bacon, sausage and eggs at a City caff.

Reed had phoned his wife, who had been only vaguely conscious of his non-appearance and was eating a Viennese breakfast with a great topping of cream in her coffee cup. Jarvis had whined to his helpmeet about an advertisement he had noticed for New Zealand lamb flaps which were nutritious and practically given away and the very thing for a couple with four children who could not, according to Jarvis, be Filled Up except at incredible expense. Now they were sitting with Superintendent Quant—his mind still filled with transvestism—and the Commander who eyed them all with a certain well-bred distaste. Old Quant, he was ruminating, should pay more attention to routine and less to buttering up the Home Office: Jarvis as usual looked like the seedier kind of abortionist's book-keeper: and Reed, his red-rimmed eyes unprotected by sunglasses, his neck thick with hairy stubble, his sixty-guinea suit wrinkled and stained, looked like nothing on earth.

It was mid-day. The snow had gone and the skies were watery grey. There was something the matter with the Commander's radiator, which emitted a dull persistent clanking. And at one o'clock he had to attend a ghastly official lunch to commemorate the merciful retirement of Superintendent Dover, whose table manners were atrocious.

"I suppose you were drunk," he shot at Reed.

"When on duty on licensed premises, sir," said that worthy round his spongy nose, "I find moderate potus desirable, otherwise one, as it were, sticks out like a sore thumb."

Christ help me, inwardly groaned the Commander, and at approximately two p.m. he would have to listen to old Harry carrying on about the ethics of police work when everybody knew he'd got away with a great slice of political graft and was the most corrupt man in the country, except for the Superintendent who now faced honourable resignation or seven years.

"And you, Mr. Jarvis, I trust will not stint yourself on the swindle sheet. We would hate to think of you being out of pocket." He was a man who liked ponderous sarcasm.

"I put in expenses as per regulations, neither more nor less," responded Jarvis with pitiless unction.

"A ship's husband might pay a wee bit out of his own pocket on occasion," said Quant, who had a rich store of clichés.

"My wife and four kids eat like horses."

"Anyway," said the Commander, "we have two corpses,

Harry Alwyn and Peter Pipchin, and a question due to be asked in the House about my efficiency."

Quant had been drearily wondering if a surtax could be put on ladies' underwear. He came to with a start and said, "What we need, Commander, is a lucky break."

"Mrs. Stoney left her country house abruptly yesterday afternoon," said the Commander, "and went to her father's old house on the river, a Dickensian fantasy of a place with a private wharf, half rotten by now, God only knows how many entrances and rat-holes in which to hide things. This morning at nine, the daughter packed up and joined her."

"I gather Mrs. Gaukroger did not like her mother that much and was prepared to double-cross her." Reed massaged a pimple.

"When the heat is on they form a united front, at least for a time. Your visit must have alarmed Mrs. Gaukroger and caused her to telephone Mama."

"Aboot those parties found on the premises after hours, though they were all clean when searched, should we charge them?" asked Quant.

"With what? Trespass? They were tacitly invited in. They were not drinking after hours at the bar. We might fineagle a charge, but how should we look in court with a gaggle of known criminals secreting themselves under the very eyes of two experienced sergeants, one of whom would be sober!"

Reed started to protest, but the Commander flapped his hand. "I guess what happened with Piper, Georgie Thigh and Johnny is that they were prospecting with a view to breaking in, but then spotted how easy it is to get lost in these ramshackle Victorian pubs. There was a case a few years ago of a family squatting in the cellarage and coming out at night to grab drink and victuals. They'd been there for some years and were only found when the sanitary inspector made a routine visit. All of which gets us no further!"

"I like Dr. Dee," said Jarvis.

The Commander's eyebrows went up. He said, slowly:

"He's never been inside except for questioning, although the Iron Curtain records are either destroyed or not available. He's naturalised, giving his place of birth as Rouen, but he is as much French as I am, which Glory Be to God I am not at all. During the War he was an agent in Paris for another doctor, Petiot by name. He contacted Jews who wanted to get to South America. Petiot took their money and murdered them. Dee was known as Monsieur Iron Fist. As you know, Petiot was discovered by the Paris Fire Brigade when his neighbours complained of the smell and for years had been protected by the Sûreté, dossiers constantly disappearing, etcetera. In the end Dr. Dee was well whitewashed and never appeared in court. He came here in 1946 and married a girl from Glasgow. She came from a criminal family and was doubly useful because she knew quite a lot of the ropes in this country—Dee's connections then were continental and North American. He's flourished pretty well, the nasty old devil, in a similar line of country to the late Harry Alwyn, except that as far as we know Alwyn never set up a robbery personally and Dee certainly does finance a lot of small but very sweet thievings. He'd be in the middle echelon, a very fit, tough old fellow indeed. Crooks do not like to offend Dee. There was a very bad beating only last year . . ."

"I remember," said Jarvis, "a man who tried to sell Dee a non-existent load of pipe tobacco. A couple of the boys flew in from Amsterdam to do it. That's on the increase and makes everything twice as difficult. I suppose it could be a foreign blow-in who killed Alwyn."

"Nobody remembers a foreigner in the pub that night," said the Commander, "though our countrymen expect them to talk like figures of fun. No, you're right, Quant, we dearly need a break."

It was in fact Sergeant Humphrey who got the break. Still feeling rather shattered after his experiences in the country, which he vowed never to visit again, Humphrey was making himself scarce, walking purposefully around with an old file on fouled footpaths under his arm. Reception was a good lurking place. A voice suddenly said at his elbow, "You're a dab at languages, Humph, and there's a lady here who only talks Irish or so I think."

The only one of his generation, his father having fled with a genial blonde when he was six, Humphrey had long been persecuted by aunts, including one who regularly, under the influence of tonic wine, dispensed good advice after sitting on her dentures. He realised that this small skinny woman was in fact yabbering in Lowland Scottish.

It had been Dr. Dee who had put the cat among the pigeons. Mrs. Dee bred the tropical fish known as *scalares*, a not inconsiderable feat, but rewarded by the spectacle of the parents teaching their young to swim. Her apparatus of pumps, heaters and tanks were in a dark room in their High-bury flat. Most of the offspring were given to unwilling friends, who bought the equipment through a firm for which Mrs. Dee was the agent, but others went to department stores. It compensated Mrs. Dee who twice a week took a fine-meshed net to a nearby pond to gather goodies for her angel fish.

That morning she had found Dr. Dee missing from the nuptial bed, a not uncommon happening as she was a heavy sleeper and the Doctor often departed stealthily during the night. On visiting her *scalares* she found that he had emptied the three breeding tanks on the carpet and was jumping on the contents.

"That fool Piper you insisted on!" he hissed.

Dumbfounded Mrs. Dee allowed her bottom jaw to gape and her husband, with astonishing alacrity, hooked out her dentures and ground them into the carpet. "Croissants, honey, KH3 and coffee in my study, and perhaps afterwards a kümmel when I ring for it!"

Meekly Mrs. Dee had prepared his breakfast, then gone quickly to the bedroom. Dr. Dee was a very slow eater, having the theory that each mouthful should be munched sixty-three times, a fact that made him a tiresome dinner guest, added to his habit of liberally ejecting any mouthful which he found trying.

Mrs. Dee packed a handful of drip-dry. By chance the Doctor had removed her jewellery from the secret safe of which he alone held the key, with a view to checking it. It was worth eight thousand pounds wholesale. This, together with twenty-five pounds housekeeping money, she stuffed in her handbag. She was out of the apartment in under twelve minutes, but she had no illusions about the curious capacities of the Doctor. "Scotland Yard," she told a bemused taxi driver, realising in panic that her words came out in a kind of mush. Mercifully, between terrified glances at the entrance to the flats, she found pencil and paper and wrote it down. Eventually she was interviewed by a suave civilian clerk who persisted in asking her how the British High Command in Ulster kept losing its equipment. Then came Sergeant Humphrey, who listened and then telephoned the Commander.

"I've got a woman here with no teeth in."

Not for nothing was the Commander forced to read old Quant's lucubrations *en route* to the Home Secretary.

"Where have you got her?" he enquired hoarsely.

"On the main reception desk, Commander."

"My God!"

"She is old Dr. Dee's wife. I'd like you to take a turn, sir, but as she has no teeth in I had better be present in case you should need assistance."

"I've only got thirty-five minutes before presenting a gold watch to a Superintendent," fairly whined his superior.

"If you could get down to it at once, we could get it over in that time, sir."

So it was that, toothless, Mrs. Dee was conducted into one of the holier of Scotland Yard Holies. The Commander, Quant, Jarvis and Reed politely got to their feet, the Commander having insisted that they remain. She was given the chair usually reserved for the Home Secretary's more important myrmidons.

"Mrs. Dee will depose, sir, that her husband was buying a quantity of stolen notes from Harry Alwyn, who was suspiciously slow in fulfilling the agreement. Dr. Dee had given a substantial deposit and it seems that this might have been his final coup before well-earned retirement to the Balearic Islands."

The Commander, who planned a retirement spent in looking at the well-developed German blondes of Mallorca while sipping brandy and discussing the yachts which never move out of the harbours, flushed with honest rage. A continental upstart daring to usurp the privileges of England! The Commander, mind half made up, wondered if the fellow was a Russian, that would delight the Foreign Office in the present circumstances. The knighthood his family coveted might be just around a corner. He asked as much.

"The Doctor is a good Roman Catholic," said Mrs. Dee, shocked at the suggestion.

What was the crazy old bugger nattering on about religion for, wondered Humphrey as he plunged gamely on. "On the day Alwyn died, Mrs. Dee heard the Doctor utter threats. 'I'll kill him, the. . . ' The noun was foreign and Mrs. Dee does not understand anything but English. All day they remained in their apartment, the Doctor drinking plum brandy, not to the extent of intoxication, but enough to key him up to what his wife calls his killer mood. Around nine he put on hat and coat and announced he was going to have it out with Alwyn. He returned at approximately three in the morning, a little drunk, and slept until the eight o'clock news which he listened to intently. Of course there was nothing on concerning the murder, but Mrs. Dee had the impression that something was very wrong."

Like other people whom circumstances have destined to silence, Mrs. Dee, the admonitory fist of the old Doctor being ten miles away (at that moment he was storming around the apartment with a warmed electric iron in his hand, which he proposed placing on Mrs. Dee's left buttock), became loquacious to the point of indiscretion, Sergeant Humphrey interpreting her gummy fulminations.

Of late, gurgled Mrs. Dee, her husband had become increasingly violent and many were the bruises she had suffered from the randy old brute.

"Unfaithful to you, missus?" enquired Jarvis. Often accusations sprang from violations of the nuptial couch— the horrid phrase was Quant's—and did not stand up in court.

That she understood and did not mind, said Mrs. Dee, a man so horny as the old Doctor having to have his wicked way. No, it was just that killing the innocent wee fish was the last straw, and in addition her teeth. No, it had come to an end between her and the Doctor, although she had wasted the best years of her life upon the wretched old brute.

"And you would get up in court and say this?" asked Quant. In his mind was the thought that this might merely be a cunning ploy. Mrs. Dee was still a well-preserved woman and Quant mistrusted such, most female murderers falling into that class. It was a time-honoured device to force the police into instigating a prosecution. Then the key witness would renege, leaving the case blown. And a person cannot be placed in jeopardy a second time.

"I would that," she said.

The Commander, who prided himself on a knowledge of difficult women from thirty years of observing the tyrant dragon he had inadvertently married, believed her, albeit reluctantly because it might be a messy kind of case to prosecute.

"The Doctor has never been convicted?" he asked.

"Not that you can prove," she averred.

That meant in practical terms that Dee could not be cross-examined as to character. The Commander groaned and phoned Records, masking his mouth with one hand. He replaced the handset and said wearily, "You were bound over for perjury at Newcastle in 1945, Mrs. Dee."

154

"It was one of my baby brothers," she gurgled. "It was my bounden duty to help the poor creature."

"Who had broken all the ribs of a street bookmaker."

"He was framed by the polis."

"Well," said the Commander, looking at his watch. It was on five to the hour and the thought of sharing the same hand towel as his table companions—the private dining-room specialised in thrift except when royalty paid a curiosity call —filled him with horror. "Now what are your own plans? Your hubby is notoriously a very choleric fellow indeed."

"The Doctor never had cholera in his life," said Mrs. Dee, "very careful with his body is the Doctor."

"I meant that if he got his hands on you you'd remember it."

"I would that, but let me get home to Glasgow and stay with my wee brothers. The Doctor's man would hardly venture there."

The Commander knew that the wee brothers, now in their forties, possessed certain powers connected with razors, and not for shaving purposes, though one was known as the Little Barber because of his expertise in severing ears. Their *fiat* carried over most of the city. Once there Mrs. Dee could defy the rage of her husband with impunity.

"We had better send you up north by police car, Mrs. Dee."

"It's kind of you, but it would do my brothers no good to have me arriving in such a way."

"For the final stage we'll have you transferred to a taxi."

For a moment the Commander pondered. Here came a crucial moment in any investigation, and the responsibility was his alone.

"Jarvis," he said, "take a short statement from Mrs. Dee, just covering the salient facts. You can do it downstairs while you are awaiting the car that Mr. Quant will arrange. You will accompany Mrs. Dee to her destination in Glasgow. It will mean that you and the driver will stay somewhere overnight."

155

Inevitably Jarvis licked his lips at the thought of a well-padded expense account, provided that he could wangle a driver of the same kidney. There was generous provision in the accountancy rules for incidentals arising from breakdowns and a shrewd man could stretch the petrol a bit.

"You and Sergeant Humphrey," the Commander addressed Reed with some distaste, "had better bring in Dr. Dee on suspicion. Mr. Quant will see him."

There was a smell of danger in Dee's experienced nostrils, to an extent which he had not known since double-crossing both Underground and Gestapo. Not that it crossed his mind that his wife might inform, but her brothers were dangerous, though he thought that they would not be stupid enough to travel south. The jewels the hag had fled away with might whet their cupidity, however, and Dee had always been at pains to conceal his true wealth, even from his wife. It might be time to disappear.

Dee ground his teeth in rage and hoped that Harry Alwyn was in hell. Contrary to his practice he poured a brandy and Benedictine, reminding himself of the unpleasant situations in which he had periodically found himself: one night in a flat in Madrid with a man dead on the floor and an accursed watchman seated on a chair before the only entrance to the block exchanging garrulous chat with the other *sereno*. He had kept his nerve and went out smoothly as the day watch arrived and bought a drink for the night man in the little *taca* opposite, but it had been a close thing and one of the many. From the secret cupboard, of whose existence Mrs. Dee was unaware, he produced the curly black wig and sticks of grease paint which to some extent changed his appearance. For three years now he had maintained a 'studio flatlet' in a big, modern warren in Fulham, as anonymous a hidey-hole as one could get anywhere today. He paid the rent by Giro and kept one of the two small wardrobes crammed with tinned food. A small overnight bag was all he needed. Into this he put papers from his safe, some of them dangerous if the police should get hold of them, his address book—the names in which read like a modern international Newgate Calendar—and a pair of brass knuckle-dusters, the latter with some reluctance because in the worst eventuality their possession almost certainly assured conviction. He cursed as he looked at his six forged passports and their accompanying identification papers. Each showed him in his wig. He selected one in the name of John Fripp, retired, aged sixty-seven, with a *residencia* card from the Spanish province of Valencia. A more pleasant thought crossed his mind as he stowed the rest back in the safe : if you had enough forged papers you were quite safe in Spain provided you kept out of the late-night bars which are police traps. He would take the Daimler and put it in for overhaul, make his way to a public lavatory and emerge as Mr. Fripp. He could remain at the flatlet for three weeks, then a couple of cautious phone calls would determine his future actions.

He was stowing eight hundred pounds in his wallet, when the front door bell rang. Swiftly, he used the peep hole. There was a large, handsome young man with large white teeth, very English and, to the Doctor's experienced eye, very police looking. He grabbed the bag and went out the kitchen entrance, realising he was not so young as he clattered down the circular iron stairway to the parking area. Prudence usually counselled him to leave the car in the open air. He switched on the heating and the motor started first time. Unable to spare the time for a warm-up, he drove smoothly on to the street and past Sergeant Reed waiting in the green police car. For a moment their eyes met. He might have anticipated this, thought Dee, but he had had no choice. In any case the police car would have to turn and his was the faster car by a long chalk. The unaccustomed drink, the excitement and the exercise of rushing downstairs had impaired his judgment, though he did not know that Reed had once been a Rally driver who specialised in bad roads and foul weather. Under foot the rain had frozen to ice and as he accelerated the Doctor felt loss of traction and perforce eased back. He turned left and the car held the road like the lady she was, but glancing in his mirror Dee saw with dismay that the green car was perhaps fifteen yards behind. Vantage was still his, for he knew the district like the back of his hand. He slowed, then swung abruptly right, gaining fifty yards as Reed stopped gingerly and backed. The Doctor chuckled. It was a straight secondary street with a bad surface, ordinarily annoying but an advantage here because it provided grip for the tyres. He put his foot down and felt the surge of horse power just as a big tanker backed out of a yard in front of him.

Dr. Dee had had no time to put on his seat belt.

"I swear to you I sounded my horn and weren't travelling more 'n two miles per," said the tanker driver to Reed five minutes later.

"He come like a bat out of hell," said his helper. " 'Watch it, Alfie,' I says and he slammed on the brakes, but the poor bleeder must have skidded because he come straight across at us. My Gawd, I thought, this little lot won't do the poor sod no good."

It demonstrably had not. An unpleasant sight in life, Dr. Dee, who had been at least partly responsible for the taking of three hundred lives in his time, made a singularly hideous corpse. The helper was dispatched to the telephone and Reed dug out his notebook.

Sergeant Humphrey, obeying orders, still had his aching forefinger imprisoning the bell button when Reed arrived half an hour later, carrying Dee's overnight bag.

"He bashed into a tanker and through the windscreen," said Reed. "Stone dead. Who'd have thought the old swine had so much blood in him!"

"Never knew you were a poetaster, Mr. Reed, I'm sure. Give us some more."

"Are you good on doors, laddie?"

"I took the course, but this 'un's really Chubby and morticed, like the old Doctor."

Reed rapped his knuckles against it.

"Sheet-metal backing," he said. "Probably an alarm setting, too. We don't want the whole ruddy neighbourhood goggling at us. Better try the back."

With tradesmen's entrances which lead into the kitchen, with its necessary window, it is generally advisable not to reinforce the door to the outside, but to concentrate upon the door leading from the kitchen to the rest of the premises. Standing beside the large rubber dustbin, Reed examined the situation. From his wallet he produced a device which looked like a cork handle with pieces of metal protruding and in a trice they were in the kitchen. In the best tradition of housebreaking Reed locked the door behind them. The entrance from the kitchen to the apartment was open, but Reed lingered and poked about. Dee had liked middle-European victuals and the big fridge was stuffed with goodies. There was expensive German beer and Reed opened a couple, taking up a bread knife to slice pieces off a leg of pork roasted with caraway seed and *gros sel*.

"The bastards do themselves proud," said envious Humphrey, whose mother blenched at the mere notion of garlic and had once fainted away in a Chinese restaurant.

"It's usually the ponces," said Reed, opening another beer can. "Burglars go for plain, healthy English nosh, and con men and embezzlers have such ulcerated guts that, apart from business, they settle for hot milk and Graham crackers. The receivers do themselves handsome and I never took in a company director who wasn't well fleshed. Of course, Dee was a foreigner and they always gorge when they've got the money. Stands to reason. Better eat it than be robbed of it tomorrow. Try the goose liver, it's rich but there's not too much of the real stuff about. It's no good letting it go to waste."

It was good, but Humphrey eyed Reed with slight

159

apprehension, for that worthy was on his third beer and there was by all evidence a lot of grog in the place. Reed was prying into cupboards and one was filled with spirits and the other with wine. Humphrey had a vision of getting the D.T.s while immured in this apartment with Reed. But the beer was wonderful, if on the heavy side, and he had another while he attacked a smoked ham.

"If this is what Ted means about the wonderful things ahead, I'm all for it," he told his colleague.

"Only the crooks will be able to afford it, lad. Well, don't stand there guzzling on duty. We've work to do. Let's have a gander into that bag."

"Preparing to bolt," said Reed at last.

"I suppose he killed Alwyn and Pipchin," said Humphrey.

"The pub is closed," said Reed, "but by appointment Dee is upstairs, waiting for a conversation. Pipchin has also lingered behind to press Gaukroger's claim, perhaps in the storeroom behind the bottle department. Dee comes downstairs when the staff have all gone and accepts a Chartreuse, which is continental when you come to think of it. There is an argument and Dee, whose mental state was on the road to insanity, whips up the bottle and smacks Harry Alwyn, leaning over the bar, squarely on the sconce. There was no time factor: he had all night to prowl around looking for the bank loot, in the course of which he finds poor cowering little Pipchin and puts out his large, mottled old maulies. Then it's Peter down the cellar and the good old Doctor back to the marriage bed."

"I see," said Sergeant Humphrey, fascinated.

"You don't see further than your spotty nose." Reed was hung-over and thus in slanderous mood, but he relented and said, "In our work, lad, a death like this is a godsend. One, we get the press off the boss's back in re Alwyn and Pipchin. Two, almost any crime on the unsolved file can be attributed to Dee."

"It doesn't seem proper."

"It's a job, a drop of free beer," said Reed, opening another, "and a pension and travelling clock at the end of the corridor. My word, real truffled pâté, and a crisp roll! Have a look through the address book while I spread it thick. Normally I don't eat of a morning, but other people's goodies whet the appetite, rather like adultery."

"He knew all the villains," finally grunted Humphrey, protruding his tongue to clear up the pâté on his upper lip. "I suppose we couldn't take away some of this food, I mean it'll only go rotten eventually."

"Ethically you are deplorable, but the rules are that you leave something for the others. There'll be a whole squad here to take the flat to bits, though I doubt that Dee kept loot here, I really do."

"Safe deposit boxes?"

"They aren't safe any more, lad, now the bankers have turned income-tax pimps by Government order. What they tend to do is take a lease on a little country cottage, some insanitary two-up-and-two-down job, and then cement it into the floor. Left-luggage offices are too much trouble, besides which the attendants co-operate with us. There are the snide solicitors, but they turn on a bit of honest blackmail. No, Dee probably has a bit of country property, the remoter the better and the rent paid six monthly from an account under the name of Jones. When the banks were snootier that could be difficult, but now it's all the 'friendly, small accounts are welcome' caper."

"Nothing that looks like an estate agency in the book, Mr. Reed, although there are three addresses for Reg Gaukroger and three for Mrs. Stoney."

"Could be a connection," said Reed, "in that Gaukroger is the changer of hot money into white by all accounts. Anyway, my boy, you put in the report because you need something to square off for sexually assaulting that old lady in Squeeze Belly Alley."

"Her complaint was nonsense!"

"And you going for Ll.B. by correspondence! I've known lads go down for three months for less. Get on the blower to Quant while I get rid of all your beer cans."

Humphrey was garrulous and Quant a compulsive whiner on the telephone, enabling Reed, a cunning look on his face, to broach a bottle of very good Scotch. When his colleague returned the evidence was concealed.

"He sounded very pleased," said Humphrey.

"He doesn't like murder cases because they take his thoughts off preventing sexual intercourse, which is his paramount task in life. The Coroner will do his duty, Mrs. Dee will shut her mouth if we are not too nosy about money, and the press will congratulate us."

"Quant said I might as well round it off by seeing Mrs. Stoney," said Humphrey. "Reg Gaukroger has disappeared, or at any rate gone to Eire to flog War Office Rejects to the I.R.A., so the Special Branch says. But Quant wants to round it off by getting back the bank loot. He thinks that if she knows where it is she might come to some settlement. There is a reward for its return, twelve thousand quid which I dare say she would get."

"You know where her house by the river is?"

"Quant is sending a car and old Fisty Harrison as driver."

Though close on retirement, 'old' Harrigan possessed certain talents by which he could and did control the best of 'em and it was a comfort to have him beside you in a car, inevitably sucking away at a peppermint.

"Nevertheless," Reed said, "by the pricking of my thumbs I counsel caution, lad. It's a bad area and the old lady has connections going back years. They used to bring the opium ashore in that area in the early twenties, and sometimes they'd find a dead 'un in the river mud, just his feet sticking out like asparagus at low tide."

"You make my blue blood curdle, Grandpa. I'd better be

on my way, because Fisty does not relish being kept waiting. Be seeing you."

The search squad could not arrive for perhaps an hour, so Reed had a final whisky before snoring off in one of the late Doctor's expensive, surgically designed armchairs. He patted the five-hundred-guinea hi-fi set-up, noted that the Doctor had preferred Mozart and went out like a light.

He dreamed of dolphins and awoke bemused and sticky mouthed. The front door bell was ringing, but he took time off to swill his face in the kitchen sink and wipe it with a beautifully embroidered tea-cloth before opening it. Three of the best searchers at the Yard stood there.

"Took your time!" said the Sergeant-in-charge, who was young, graduated from Cambridge and did not approve of Reed, dishevelled and stinking of liquor.

"It's a very special door," said Reed, "and it took me a bit of time to open it."

"Hm, yes she is a beauty. Have you any ideas?"

"All negative. Dee was too old a dog to keep much here in the way of jewellery or hot notes. There is a safe, but," he fumbled in the pocket of his crumpled suit, "here are his keys. The safe has two locks and no combination, a straight-forward job with no booby traps or alarm. Well, I'll wait in the kitchen. Just call if you want me."

Reed made himself useful with Mrs. Dee's coffee pot and ham sandwiches.

"The safe is stacked with false papers and passports, which I wonder why he didn't take," said the Sergeant-in-charge.

"Does you no good," said Reed, bored. "If one is not enough, seven are not, and if you get pulled in on suspicion, it's a dead give-away." He collected the empty cup and plates from the top of the hi-fi equipment. No point in leaving too much mess.

Reed washed up neatly, put the beer cans down the disposal chute, and took the overnight bag to the living-room. "I'm knocking off," he said. "This bag belonged to Dee and you already have his keys. There was stuff in his breast

163

pocket, but I left that for the experts at the morgue. So long!"

Fisty Harrigan was a tall, fairish man with a battered face, not that he ever provoked a fight. However in his twenty-nine years of police work he had never avoided one. Colleagues were dubious about his intelligence overall, but certain of his loyalty, tenacity and low cunning. He slid the police car into the kerb two minutes after Humphrey's arrival, whining and snuffling through his broken nose in approval of his punctuality.

"Reed thinks there might be trouble, Fisty," said Humphrey as they made off. It was getting dark.

"Animals around there," wheezed Fisty. "And the old lady's mother came from the district. The family used to shanghai sailors when the going was good—the Australian run mostly." He sucked broken, blackened teeth in contemplation of ancient sins. It was close on five and for the next hour he stolidly fought traffic, the interior of the car getting hotter and fustier, for Harrigan was no believer in fresh air.

A return of boyhood car sickness, or perhaps the goose liver, impelled Humphrey to close his eyes, to embark upon a dark turbulent personal sea punctuated by waves which threatened to capsize him totally. The sweat on his brow was clammy when he felt the car stop and the merciful lavage of ice-cold air when he inhaled.

"Feeling sick, boy? Would you like me to call in a few of the locals?" Fisty was mildly contemptuous and indignation spilled into Humphrey's mind.

"It's that I get car sick."

"A woman's complaint," snorted Harrigan, who had turned off his lights. "See that down below, that was Mrs. Stoney's father's house, not that he lived there."

In the darkness was silhouetted a house with two floors and two chimneys. A solitary light meandered rather than shone through one downstairs window.

"Most of it is blacked out with roller blinds. There are a couple of comfortable rooms and a kitchen. The rest, sixteen rooms altogether, are just empty."

"I take it you've been round it, Fisty?"

Harrigan closed one cold blue eye. "And how should we molest an influential, moneyed old Queain like Mrs. Stoney, with the finest lawyers in London at her purse string, the old cow? It so happened that Mr. Quant thought we might one day want a bit of a plan of the place so he arranged for the local fire inspector to make a visit with yours truly tagging along to hold the tape measure. I made a sketch of it and refreshed me memory before I left Victoria Street tonight. A funny old place is that house, with a bit of it right over the river at high tide and a nasty-looking trapdoor with the rankest stink of Thames mud I encountered in years. There was nothing illicit there, though you wouldn't know the hidey-holes. There was an old rat of a caretaker, a rheumatic snarly cove who used to be one of the boys until the river air got him. There's still a bit of stuff which comes in here-abouts, jewellery and furs, essences of perfume and liqueurs, but the big stuff is gone. Radar, the new launches and heli-copters scared the operators off years ago. But a tidy bit of money comes in for the locals to keep 'emselves pissed on, and they're still the same sullen inbred lot they were a hun-dred years ago. If you want to hole up you can be safe here for a price and maybe get false papers and a steward's job on a freighter. Well, you know we haven't got a warrant?"

"Quant doubted we had a case that would stand up to enquiries."

"Bloody old woman! Well, we'll have to mag ourselves in. The old 'did you hear anything funny last night' approach. There might be trouble. If they are too accommodating watch it. Well, I've given them time to settle. It's when you burst in unexpected that you get a lead injection."

"You think they *know* we're here?"

"Be your age, sonny boy. They knew we were here five effing minutes ago," said Fisty, "but they couldn't bolt because I can see the exits now my eyes are accustomed to the dark."

The big man had the reputation of seeing like a fox, thought Humphrey sullenly as he followed his bulk, partly by the peppermint spoor, across treacherous broken concrete and then worm-eaten board.

"The door's here," said Fisty, not troubling to lower his voice. He drew back one stout boot and kicked thunderously. Eventually there came the sound of a laborious drawing of bolts.

"Who are you?" asked a rather hoarse voice, as though the subject had a cold.

"Police seeking information from honest citizens," said Harrigan.

"You've come to the right place," said the voice. "Wipe your feet before tramping it into the Axminster."

They went into the narrow, brown-painted hallway with its strip of worn lino, and dirt-covered twenty-five-watt bulb. "My ladies are in the great salon," camped their conductor in butler-like travesty. Peering past Harrigan Humphrey could only see longish black hair and a glimpse of long curling side whiskers. He had seen the fellow before. Of course, it had been at Reg Gaukroger's party, the night the bed had collapsed. The Sergeant recoiled at the memory, realising suddenly that as life went on he was getting plenty of memories to recoil from. There were various doors with peeling paint at intervals along the corridor and a larger, hand-carved portal at the end which in the gloom he thought might be teak.

The man opened it with a flourish. "Two police gents to visit the gentry," he proclaimed. Humphrey thought he caught the herbal whiff of smoked resin. From whatever source their guide was slightly high.

Brought up in a modest generation which had closed whore-houses except in Perth, Western Australia, where the climate becomes very sultry and there are a lot of citizens of Mediterranean stock, Humphrey thought the room they went into might have been the waiting-room for a genteel Victorian sporting house, with a crinoline-clad lady presiding over the rituals. Mrs. Stoney wore a maxi skirt of forbidding aspect, and Mrs. Gaukroger a green pyjama suit. The daughter *had* something, telegraphed the Sergeant's glands, and as his scoutmaster had taught him he thought of railway engines.

"Well?" asked Mrs. Stoney.

"Did you hear anything strange in the night, ma'am?" asked Harrigan.

"One is not accustomed to hearing strange things in the night," the lady answered, her face composed in scorn.

"Even if we might have heard things going bump, we were not here last night, having arrived at the ancestral mansion this morn," said Mrs. Gaukroger, frankly grinning.

"You must realise ladies that this is, well, one might say a toughish area and it is the bounden duty of the police to afford citizens the protection for which, after all, they pay . . ." Sweating slightly, Fisty stood there reciting great gobs of *Gideon's Concise Guide for the Moral Direction of Young Officers*, a thousand copies of which* were reputed to be flushed down loos each spring.

Humphrey thought he caught a sidelong glint from the massive constable's cold eyes. The male factotum had parted the curtains over the window and was conducting some kind of peering operation. The ladies had their shrewd faces turned upwards to Harrigan. The penny dropped. There was another door to the room, standing wide open, which accounted for the draught on his ankles and the flickerings of the large gas fire. Stealthily he shuffled sideways and through it.

It was dark and smelled of mouse dirt and old cheese. Hellish dark, thought Humphrey, and why old buildings either smell of cheese or ancient cabbage he had never fathomed. He had forgotten his pencil torch and damned

* On personal application to Mr. Harold Macmillan at his club.

his mother who had insisted he changed his suit at the last moment of departing for work. Humphrey adored his mama, but he did wish that the loving, portly lady would not do things like spitting on her handkerchief and rubbing his cheek with it. At first the light from the salon showed him what appeared to be a series of little rooms, each leading from the other. It must go back to 1820, thought Humphrey who knew something of architecture, probably a pub where the bosses paid off the casual river labour and a crib for sailors who had jumped ship. He felt the prickle of old evil and it was very cold. For light he was driven back upon his cigarette lighter which became almost too hot to hold, but the rooms were deserted and he thought he saw a couple of rats shrinking back into darkness. He went through six doors before finally coming upon a larger one with peeling pink wallpaper covered with red roses, the lot surmounted by a greenish mould. There were plump suitcases on the floor, and he counted twelve before his lighter gave a tiny belch and expired. True to training Humphrey stretched out his arms and inched towards the nearest wall. He imagined he felt the oozing damp as he stood against it, for by his calculation this room must jut over the black, dismal pollution of the Thames, where once salmon had sported and oysters pursued their somnolent life. His phosphorescent watch dial showed him that it was six minutes since he had left the salon and he was uncertain what to do. He supposed that he could retrace his steps: there seemed to be a tiny flicker of light at the end of the blackness though it might have been his eyes playing tricks. Then he thought of Fisty Harrigan's silent contempt if he came creeping back, with so little accomplished and with the lame excuse of not having his torch with him. It would get around and finally reach Authority, these things always did. For want of something better, he sidled along the wall, rubbing the back of his outstretched hand up and down the slimy wallpaper. Presently he felt wood and a door handle, he twisted and pulled and was greeted by a smell like rotting paper.

He got the door fully open, then froze as the back of his neck prickled. A brief flash of torchlight blinded him before a skilled chop at the side of his neck paralysed him and he was shoved through the door, which was slammed behind him. On his knees, Humphrey had the feeling that several people were pressing against him. Something flapped over his head and he let out a neighing cry for help as his heart raced. The paralysis abated and he lashed out, feeling his knuckles tear on metal. Sheer fear drove him down like a spent horse. It smelled bad, but he was lying on something soft. He strugged to his feet and sought a door handle, but only the smooth surface of wood greeted his fingertips. Humphrey sank to his haunches and stared into the blackness.

CHAPTER SEVEN

"In a way, I'm sorry for the lad," said Quant to the Commander next morning, "for they canna help themselves. It's like bees around the sugar bowl."

"Victorian corsets, you said?" observed the Commander as though it made matters worse.

"It's a ver' old place," said Quant, "and this old wardrobe or closet hadn't been opened for years. On the floor were bits of *Reynolds News* dated 1882. When the search party found him at six a.m., myself having become worried at an absence of any report, he had, let me see . . ." the Superintendent donned horn-rims . . . "he had two pairs of whalebone corsets draped over his head. Others had apparently been torn at with what the local Inspector, who has a degree from University College, thinks was sexual frenzy and his back and neck were reposing upon two pairs of ladies' drawers, the ones under his neck having pink lace on them. He was incoherent. Constable Harrigan, who had been coshed, bound and gagged in the drawing-room, said he merely indicated to Humphrey that he should take a quiet look at the place. A judge would not approve, but he would probably admit the evidence if it was relevant. Humphrey was searched, in case a complaint is laid, and he had no torch, which is against regulations. He said he had lost it. Well, sir, do I apply for a warrant to apprehend Mrs. Stoney and her daughter?"

"And for God's sake on what evidence? Harrigan did not see who hit him and Humphrey was clawing off ladies' stays!"

"Now, sir, taking 1880 as the criterion, the ladies would have to be over eighty and even Lord Borrage, who one fears has become senile, could hardly let that go to a jury!"

"Mrs. Gaukroger might wear old corsets for kicks," said the Commander, remembering his repulsive eldest daughter's desire to garb herself in eighteenth-century naval garb, common sailors' too, not even officers'.

"You don't travel by Underground in the hot months, sir. Corsets are definitely out among the ladies. It's the men . . ." Quant faded out remembering that the Commander's growing bulk was controlled by something more than prayer and nature.

"I do not know what we can do with Humphrey, sir," continued Quant. "A recommendation for bravery* and a brilliant summation of the Alwyn-Pipchin murders to present to the Coroner. Records tell me that there are at least thirty-four major cases to be written off against Dr. Dee. And he cannot—" Quant permitted himself the slightest of official smirks—"rebut them."

The Commander's wife had lately taken up spiritualism and he was none too sure that the unpleasant Doctor would not reach over with rappings, phosphorescent appearances and automatic writing, spitefully blowing the gaff from the other world. But he was familiar with the time-honoured gambit of piling unsolved cases upon the dead.

"Is there any risk of this fellow Humphrey ripping clothes off women while on duty? What he does in his spare time I don't care."

"He has a fiancée," said Quant primly.

"Curse his fiancée! You're the expert."

"It's clothes lines and wardrobes and sometimes Marks and Spencer stores, sir. I've done quite a bit of reading about it, though there was a case of a young lady, travelling by slow train to Birmingham, who awoke on June 7th, 1929, without her nether garments. Sergeant Appleby, as he was then, put in a report saying that it was probably a jest by some students who were travelling on the train. Krafft-Ebing says it is quite vicarious, but I advise that we annotate

* The Odds on Death (Gollancz).

171

his file to the effect that he must be kept under strict supervision and away from women. And of course no further promotion."

The Commander, who had a vague idea that Krafft-Ebing was the revolting but economical cheese served at home when the guests were unimportant, nodded his head. Just then the intercom buzzed. "It's Humphrey reporting in," he groaned, leaning over to one of Quant's hairy ears, "shall I have him up?"

"Better get it over with, sir."

They sat gloomily for six minutes while Humphrey came up in the overworked lift. A generally eupeptic young man, he had rushed home, soothed his mother who had not Slept a Wink, twittered amiably to his unconcerned fiancée by telephone, snatched an hour's sleep, showered and was now flashing his white teeth with the best of them. The Commander did not offer him a chair, and thinking this was oversight, the Sergeant helped himself.

"You are quite all right, Mr. Humphrey?" The Commander pushed a cautious pawn forward.

"I was very dizzy, sir, but the family doctor who my mama phoned up said it was probably slight asphyxia, the closet having a tight-fitting door. It was oak, they tell me, and three inches thick."

"You're the first man I ever heard of who was slightly asphyxiated by ladies' corsets," said the Commander in a flash of temper.

"They made merry quips on that in the police car," said Humphrey, the three sausages and two eggs digesting comfortably in his stomach. "I was dead scared they were bats."

"Bats!" The Commander smiled malevolently.

The top bits of brass were quaint old daddy-o's, thought Humphrey. All idiosyncrasy and eccentricity, but with damned good hearts underneath. He wondered if the Commander would anounce a step-up verbally, or write him a fatherly letter.

Goddam the young bastard, the Commander was thinking sourly. He'd probably gorged himself on a morning fry-up. The Commander recalled dismally his own raw egg and milk done in the blender, for even that nowadays had the power to tweak his duodenum. "You have no idea who pushed you into that closet?"

"I had dropped my pencil torch," lied Humphrey, "but had opened the door. There was a flash from a torch, a blow on the left of my neck and I found myself inside and the door shut. I had not even a glimpse of whoever it was, man or woman, but they knew what they were doing all right."

"How is your neck?" asked the Commander with deceptive casualness.

"Not a mark, sir," replied Humphrey cheerfully, "no bruising at all, just a very slight stiffness if I turn my head hurriedly. How is Harrigan?"

"Bad tempered, but with a nasty bruise, probably from a sandbag wielded quite expertly on the top of the spine. You can kill with that if you haven't taken lessons. As it is he'll be in an observation ward for a few days, but he saw nobody as he was trying to get the two women talking. When he came to, he was expertly trussed."

"He was gagged," interposed Quant, "and with the thick walls of the house he had no chance of making himself heard."

"There was no danger, and probably no intent to injure," continued the Commander. "The police car was left in plain sight, though the local inhabitants had stolen the four wheels, part of the engine, and looted the inside, Harrigan having omitted to lock it. I cannot blame him. In the case of an arrest, which he anticipated might be the case, you don't want to be fiddling with keys, certainly not in that district. And stupid, incompetent and idle as my staff is," the Commander's neck reddened with fury and spleen, "they would hardly overlook the non-return of two men from an assignment."

Quant kept a discreet silence, doodling corsets on his

scratch pad. He was a fair draughtsman. Humphrey twittered brightly, "I suppose we're insured."

The Commander paused, then said, "No, my boy, we are not insured and there will be a preliminary enquiry, a Home Office enquiry, an Auditor General's enquiry, and approximately two tons of paper-work. But thank you for the kindest of thoughts. I was leading in my clumsy way to the fact that we have no evidence at all concerning the assault upon Harrigan, and your own soporific experience amid ladies' garments."

Humphrey guffawed. What a jolly old cock it was, to be sure! He must tell his mother an expurgated edition. On second thoughts he remembered how his mother looked after one of her splurges on hot scones, a healthy English diet in her estimation, and diagnosed indigestion. He wondered whether he should mention his mother's great-auntie's specific, consisting of peppercorns and bay leaves, but decided the moment was not opportune. Perhaps when he got his step up to Inspector ... "I did report that Mr. and Mrs. Gaukroger's manservant was in the room."

"Aye," said Quant, "one Chas. Comfrey, aged thirty-five, born in Bow, approved school at eleven, two years for breaking and entering, three years for being found in a warehouse, and four years for burglary. A whiff of violence about him but nothing proven, just the rumour among his peers that Charlie is not the boy to push too hard. A smarmy type who worked himself on to the catering staff while in prison. Sometimes when he was out he took a job as a waiter or barman. Our files say he lost his taste for being inside, as they do, and was content to be a jackal of Gaukroger. He lived in, dropped the usual pro haunts. Men like Gaukroger need toughish staff who won't talk, just in case an emergency happens."

The Commander fingered a bit of paper from the flimsy pile in one of his baskets. "There was a launch going down stream at midnight. All in order, run by a small pleasure-cruise company with a smell about it. Ten to one Mrs. Stoney, her daughter and the tough boy were on it. Plus loot of course, though what happened to the bank haul is something of which I am increasingly doubtful. We have written it off to Dr. Dee. Anyway they'll have transferred on to some small freighter going to one of the 'no questions asked if you have the money' ports. Plenty of them nowadays and as long as the democratic officials get their cut you may sell your auntie, dentures and all. Pah! The Conservatives have the right idea, make them colonies again with a Governor who'll stand no nonsense. Look at the Australians, creating violent scenes on rugger pitches, and their Parliament doin' nothing!" The Commander had for years hankered after a Governorship in a small, warm country with obedient, clean natives, but they were getting as scarce as hens' teeth and he supposed he would have to settle for a life peerage when the time came. He flinched from a dyspeptic pang and Humphrey concluded that this patriotic old dug-out was remembering his dead comrades of yesteryear who had defied the Mahdi or Sadat or somebody like that who didn't play fair.

"And now, Sergeant!" The Commander's tones were silk soft.

"Here it comes," thought Humphrey and rigidly stretched his back until he felt something give.

"A Mr. Bill Botting is a Chief Inspector of the Boy Scout Movement. He complains that while the boys are out on their healthy rambles, hippies, by which I gather he means everybody who is not actually completely bald, break into their club houses and purloin wrist watches, civilian clothes, etcetera. Mr. Botting being insistent that time should be told by the sun, or the stars as the case may be, a lot of watches are left at the club houses and the looting is considerable. Insurance companies refuse to insure Boy Scouts for reasons that your Sunday reading will provide. You will procure the file and take over the case."

Humphrey snapped to attention, and restrained himself from clicking his heels. Some kind of subtle test was involved here, he was sure. "Immediately, sir, or as the Spans say *muy pronto*"—no harm in reminding 'em that you were a linguist. He flashed his teeth, beamed and was off.

"Are you sure he'll be safe with Boy Scouts?" whined Quant as the door closed.

"They don't bloody well wear corsets. I thought you said it was women's underclothes!"

"There are Girl Guides, sir, some of them quite elderly."

"Mr. Botting is a very sound, modest man, Quant. He has forbidden his Scouts to associate with the Girl Guides and is even very careful about fauna, believing that rabbits and the like might induce dangerous thoughts in conjunction with TV. His boys specialise in botany. Can't go wrong with flowers, eh?"

Quant was not so sure, but sighed and said, "We turn to the body found in the Headquarters of Women's Lib., sir."

The Commander groaned.

His wife had spoken of a good old-fashioned Viennese lunch and hastened out to buy double cream so Sergeant Reed wrote a note to the effect that he was urgently called away, switched off the tape-recorder and crept down the tradesmen's stairs. He decided not to take his car. It was ten and he was feeling suspiciously fit, a condition which inevitably presaged a king-size hangover the following morning. However it was to be savoured, and the Sergeant had confined himself to an ice-cold quart bottle of ale, gulped down before making his escape, instead of his usual kümmel and coffee. The weather had achieved a typical swing-up in temperature. The sludge had gone and the sun looked like a lightly poached egg. Reed's matutinal belchings mingled pleasantly, to his ears, with the soft mutterings of the drains. He stopped at a snack bar and had grilled ham and coffee, providing a bed upon which the libations ahead could happily float. He made his way leisurely by bus to Victoria and thence to the briefing room.

"You're not listed as on," said the man on the door.

"I cannot keep away, crime fascinates me like a candle does a moth."

"I thought it was beer," grunted his old friend. "On the pub murder, weren't you, you lucky old sod?"

"Having supported 'em all these years I deserved the break."

The 'running file' on Alwyn and Pipchin was marked 'to be closed after the Inquest'. Reed went through it, from his own, first report, to that from the squad who released Humphrey and Harrigan. Silly young bastard to let himself be pushed into a cupboard! He was not displeased on the whole, but ... The Sergeant sighed and stood there in thought.

"Are you on, Mr. Reed?" It was a harried-looking inspector whose life was spent detecting people who fiddled their electric or gas meters. His eyes had brightened upon seeing a sergeant with nothing to do.

"Off, just came in to take a gander at the Alwyn murder file."

"Oh." The Inspector's slant on life was strictly metrical. Murders bored him to tears.

Reed mooched off to a pub near Piccadilly where was sold porter in chi-chi surroundings at a price which would have made a Dubliner faint. He savoured the black brew with a thick ham sandwich in the other hand. It was with some reluctance that he caught a taxi to the Admiral Byng, arriving there at twelve thirty in time to see the earlier City birds, a few fugitives from Fleet Street, and an indubitable tour from Buffalo, being given a treat before goggling at Mr. Bolt's latest offering. They must be doing land-office business, he thought as he watched Mr. Pudding at work on the tourists. In one of his abrupt character changes the Brewery representative had assumed the aspect of a showman in front of a fat lady, or the less pleasing type of travel agent. He was attended by the hairy courier, a young man who looked as if he had been slightly hanged.

"Well, I mean," the courier whined in his Leeds accent, "about the Bard there is no actual evidence he ever came here, but doubtless, I mean, his friends ... heavy topers, what?"

"O Rare Ben Johnston!" Mr. Pudding sighed and removed his bowler hat.

"It's too early for food as far as I am concerned," said the little old lady who was the interlocutor, "but I'll go along with it. Steak, I suppose. I understood the young man was saying this is a criminal haunt."

"See him!" Him was a fascinatingly seedy man, with a huge diamond impaled to his purple cravat and scars all over his face. His eyes twitched between the clock and the door. The make-up was overdone, decided Reed, recognising a jovial actor who played men who molested children.

"If I told you what he's done, ma'am," continued Pudding in a ghastly whisper, "your blood would run ice-cold."

"Now see here, I'm from Buffalo, my dear sir, and we got the Mafia there."

Mr. Pudding's jaw dropped.

"Now, Mrs. Peten, you know the President himself has banned that word because there ain't no such thing." A jowly man with a black stubbly chin glared indignantly.

"Nobody banned it that I heard. It's truth, Mr. Ginistrelli."

The courier raised his voice to a shrill trumpeting. "All members of Conn's Comfy Caravanserai for Educational Pleasure! Where's Mrs. Murphy? Mrs. Murphy! I didn't see you, madam, because of the pillar. Now we will have a cold collation of delicious viands, prepared from traditional recipes by loving hands. Follow me, please, the toilets are on the right."

"They buy any drinks?" asked Reed.

Mr. Pudding shrugged as he raised a finger to Joe Pollick. "All teetotallers except the Italian and Mrs. Murphy, but it pays at contract price. One Martini or national drink as they call it and a tomato juice allowed at the bar. Brewery

Mead at the table, that always gets them in. It took our chemists nine years to find a substitute for honey. Some fool started writing to the papers claiming it killed rats. My Chairman went him scone-hot, pointed out personally to the Editors that we had no rats in our establishments. I did hear that the lunatic lost his job and is now a traveller for a firm of rodent operators, which shows you that there is a Destiny that shapes our whatsits. A little service, there, Mr. P., it wouldn't suit my Chairman if he had to wait. A b. and b., Sergeant Uh, with the first b. from my private bottle."

There was a slight tell-tale clink as Pollick, seamy faced, but with his new suit recently pressed, poured. New authority, which can be nerve-racking, plus hard drink, diagnosed Reed idly. He'd have to get over it or get out. A man built like a barrel, all chest, jaw and steely eyes, suddenly strutted in from the public and glared around. "One of Agatha Christie's stalwarts," said Mr. Pudding, "and what he gets *per diem* staggered my Chairman. More than the Commissioner at your show, so he worked it out. But ain't he a perfect sleuth? Look at the cunning way he's got the cuffs peeping out of one pocket and a bloodstained hanky out of the other. At home he does wonderful *petit point*, which is a kind of crochet or suchlike, which is funny considering his appearance. He'll arrest the spiv type at ten minutes before closing tonight. There'll be a bit of a scuffle and the gyvves will be snapped on. We'll have a car waiting outside with a lot of flashing lights on it. Ah, well, I must take a dekko at the dining-room."

It filled up rapidly. Reed drained his drink, which he did not much like, opted for half a pint of best bitter to take the taste away, winced at its chemical flavour (this year the Brewery chemists, flouncing about in their white coveralls, were on to a substitute for hops) and stood against the wall.

Automatically he noted that the pressure of bodies had forced a reluctant stockily built man to his side. He was Father Hopcraft, a slum landlord who augmented his meagre rents in strange and unlawful ways.

"Not often you're this side of the river, Father."

"There was a fellow to meet me," said Hopcraft, palpably lying, "what hasn't turned up. The yunkers have no sense of time, Ser'nt."

"On account of the hash you sell 'em."

Red-currant eyes in little bags of lard flickered at Reed. "You must have your little joke."

Hopcraft was a largish jackal. If he got on to something big he 'sold it upstairs' as the saying went, taking his five per cent, but on occasions fenced quite large hauls on his own account, some of the condemned, dismal hovels he owned doubling as excellent hiding places. It was strange, Reed thought, how the crooks were gathering around the Admiral Byng. Anyhow it was none of his business, so he gossiped about the Common Market, not the one pontificated upon in the Commons, but a rather more efficient idea whereby a fast-moving European criminal association would be formed. Already Belgian burglars, cameras hung over their shoulders, lounged in at Heathrow and, the job accomplished, returned two days later, their bags innocently filled with cheap English clothes and butter.

"We put the Eyeties in their place," sighed Hopcraft, "and the Krauts are reasonable as always, particularly on the point of giving up kicking people so much. But it's the French, you can't do nothing with them. The 'oring business which they was so good at has gone off because the tourist trade 'as dropped and the girls sit around quacking 'O mong jew, la la' all day, eating their heads off. And as for thievery, an honest thief can't get a living. A smart hotel boy I know, specialises in getting in the open transom windows, had his suitcase with the tools taken five minutes after getting into Gare du Nord, and by an amateur, an old lady what should know better. Two hundred thousand quid subsidy, guaranteed, is what the French Heads demand. They say if we bolster up their 'oring industry we can have a share of the Marseilles heroin factories, but I don't fancy paying a contrib of five hundred quid a year, particularly not speaking

French. I wish we 'ad a man with Mr. 'Eath's brains to advise us."

"They're a ropy lot and in a bad way, especially since the Danes and Yanks reefed the porno bit off them," agreed Reed.

"My uncle," said Hopcraft almost tearfully, "made a livin' flogging *Lady Chat,* printed in Cairo, around Calais. Twenty years he was at it until Penguins went and ruined it all. I have to make him an allowance; that's progress for you."

"Cut the cackle, Father." Reed momentarily trod hard on the man's instep. "It's the bank loot, isn't it? Before you answer have a little think. We've always been fair to you and you've been fair to us, our different jobs considered. But there's another side to me, Father. If I take a dislike to a man, I make his life a bother. Oh, dear, yes, until he wishes he was dead or inside for forty years, which is where in fact he lands. It won't hurt you to sing a little, and you'll have read that Dr. Dee has gone to his rest."

"It gets so *difficult,*" mourned Hopcraft. "Take my dad who had a sweetie shop in Wapping. Coves used to come in and say 'Wot will you give me for this, Mr. 'Opcraft?', dockies mostly, and dear old dad used to treat them fair so that when he joined the Great Majority he had thirty terrace houses in good repair and an interest in six well-run knocking shops, God rest his soul. We have six masses a year said for him."

Having heard a few reminiscences—Reed was a repository for the memories of all the retired old bores who still hung around—of Hopcraft senior, Reed privately thought that several thousand years of entreaty would be needed to improve his theological position at the going rate.

"It was only towards the end he even paid income tax, Ser'nt. Fancy that now! And poor me with three accountants, one full time." Hopcraft lowered his voice. "The bank loot's still floatin'. In the perfesh nobody got 'ide nor 'air of it."

"Sure?"

"Gard! I *know*. It's a kind of club that we've got. If somebody's bought loot it's no good the rest of them flattening their trotters running around trying to bid for it. But Alwyn, or so he said," a twinge of doubt passed over the stout man's face, "had it and was for passing it on, but he was rare twisty about it and they say he delivered brummy notes a couple of times. That's bad. You want to know who done him in! Now remember this to my credit, Ser'nt, the Heads was calling a meeting about Harry. After all if we don't have our *intergity* as Sir Alec would say, 'ow are we to face the new challenges ahead? Harry might have got the verdict against him at the meeting and one of the German boys brought over to settle him under the new interim arrangement. But he was croaked days before the meeting, which was fixed for last night. It's *tejus* getting everyone together, the Scotch boys not liking to cross the border an' all. You can take my word for it that his death weren't organised."

"What about Mrs. Stoney and Dr. Dee?"

"They were invited to the meeting. It was a bit tricky with the old lady, on account of her daughter and Harry, but when it's business the old grey mare don't flinch from the whip. But it didn't come to that. Old Dee hated Alwyn!"

"And why are you here?"

"He lived here and was killed here. When you fish you go to a well-stocked pool. I might as well spend a few hours here watchin' faces."

"What faces?"

"Anybody's. In my game, like yourn, you get instinck, a kind of eighth sight like. If I see A talking to B, and C walks in, then perhaps I put two and two together."

"And the result will be g-a-o-l and seven if you keep on quacking at me like an old whore," snarled Reed, upset because somebody had nudged his drinking arm.

Alarmed, Hopcraft tried to sidle away, but Reed's free hand clutched his shoulder. "Look Ser'nt," said the fence, "how did it leave the premises, a nice fat bunch of hay like that? We worked it out he must have stoushed it here."

"It was searched by experts," grunted Reed, nevertheless perturbed. "And some of the boys had a go the other night, folk like Mr. Tupper and Big Bertie, who find gramophone needles in haystacks."

"Did they look on the roof, fer instance?"

"How the bloody hell do I know where they looked? It's a pitched roof, so who's going to crawl around on it concealing banknotes? Any case, this London rain will rot a brass monkey, let alone paper. Your brains are going, friend. When you get inside I'll see you're put in the old stupids' wing and get plasticine to play with. Or beads." Reed put his empty glass on the narrow shelf and bullocked his way to the street. There was a slight drizzle and the buildings looked uglier than ever against a lowering sky.

A hundred yards away was a tea shop, where he got himself what purported to be roast beef and probably had been at one stage of its career, but that was some time ago. The shop was filled with dismal men and smelled of wet wool. What appetite he had quickly vanished, but the coffee substitute was at least hot and sweet. He got out his thick notebook and brooded over it. Not one gloomy face took the slightest notice, he was perfectly anonymous. The happy Jamaican ladies at the servery, steam drifting into their broad faces, clattered away with their implements. Viennese food or not, Reed suddenly felt old and wished he was at home. He pushed his coffee away and went into the street.

As she told him, avid for gossip, Mrs. Crippen, cleaner extraordinary at the Admiral Byng, kept herself to herself, a state developed by having brought up eight children in the two rooms she occupied. The rooms, littered though they were with foam mattresses, were scrupulously clean and polished, even down to Mrs. Crippen's prized collection of china owls. The family was out, even himself, who 'minded' barrows in the street market while their owners had a 'wet' in the pub over the road. Some chips on a piece of newspaper and a slight odour of fried fish provided evidence that the lady had lunched early.

"What about the jools I found?" asked the amiable crone, cracking a swollen thumb joint in a way that got on Reed's nerves. "When Crippen licked 'is lips and said we should take a pub, I give him *my look* to shut him up. A fish-and-chips, I says, 'cause you carnt get pissed on 'em even if you get down on the vinegar."

"You'll have to wait a couple of months," said Reed. "They probably won't be claimed, although ten to one they are stolen property from God knows where."

"Course," said Mrs. Crippen amiably, "the gaffer being a fence there must have been stolen goods about, not that I thought he handled 'em personal so that it could be proved."

"You knew he was a fence?"

"Everybody did," she replied. "'Arry Alwyn the fence, likewise Farver 'Arry."

"First I heard that it was generally known among the staff," grumbled Reed.

"Live and let live, ducky, and if yer keep yer mouth closed nobody's going to stick a 'ot tater down yer gullet."

"I'd like to ask you a few questions, my old dear."

"The point is," said Mrs. Crippen, "that I don't want a 'ot tater down my gullet, nor my old mug massaged with a razor, nor bein' snubbed by my old mates when I toddle over for me pint of stout and a bit of Welsh rabbit."

"What I'm asking is innocent enough, so let's have a sit-down and a chat, and to lubricate the old uvula this." From an inside pocket he whipped a quartern of brandy, enough for two stiff tots.

The apprehensive look passed from Mrs. Crippen's face as she registered the label and ogled it.

"I'll get the glasses," she said. "Them bloody toothbrushes the kids stick in 'em drive you crackers, plus Crippen's falsies which he won't wear because of 'is tender gums."

*   *   *

There was a recital of Mozart performed by four Austrians and Reed made it with five minutes to spare, and sat dreaming he was in Salzburg seated on the flimsy-looking gold chairs in the old palace listening to Mozart being played like some Byzantine rite. For the umpteenth time he made the resolution to take more of his music live, but knew he would not keep it. As he left a wind with a bitter bite about it had sprung up and Reed huddled into his second-best coat. He went and had a chop and afterwards strolled round the half-dozen small clubs which were on his assignment list. Here forgathered the cashiered ex-jockeys, the small bookies, the tipsters and hangers-on who constituted the 'racing boys'. They knew Reed, all except the newest of recruits, and accepted him with resignation. If it was not the plump Sergeant it would be another, perhaps more deadly, so they hardly dropped their voices although they lapsed into the obscure, changing argot of their profession when he came too near. Ten per cent of them were well, even nattily dressed, but the remainder dropped rapidly down the scale to threadbare coats and watchless wrists. At his penultimate call, Reed found the man he wanted, a tough man, but less tough than he looked, a collector of gambling debts. He could be hired to bellow on front doorsteps or to penetrate into the business premises of some shivering clerk, there to berate him. He had a nice line of patter, filled with allusions to English sportsmen, honourable dealings and paying one's debts. Sometimes wives realised that with little difficulty he could be chased off the premises, for he had a horror of physical assault. For three gins he focused his ruined vocal chords upon Reed and gave him information which made the Sergeant frown.

In spite of the cold it was invigorating weather to be walking in, and he enjoyed watching the lowered-headed scuttlings of the less hardy folk he encountered and the feel of his breath as the wind took it and changed it to steamy vapour. A spot at the top of his nose began to hurt and his ears were numb by the time he reached the Admiral Byng shortly before closing time.

The evening had apparently been a success. The crowd were contentedly bibulous, apart from one red-faced man who was complaining to Mr. Pudding about a tear in his coat pocket.

"All good friends and jolly good company," Mr. Pudding was suggesting, " and come, sir, I noticed it was torn when you came in."

"That's right," came the seconding voice of Joe Pollick, a trifle thickly.

Reed drifted through the thinning crowd. When sober, as he was, he was adept at 'losing himself', a useful criminal and police skill. He passed the snack bar, now a mass of half-eaten food and dirty glasses. The door to upstairs was in an alcove. Reed leaned against it and with his hand behind his back ascertained that it was locked. His probing forefinger caressed the old-fashioned surface of the front plate. From his pocket he produced a wallet and selected a tool that looked halfway between a bagging needle and a fish hook. Once more he groped behind him, this time for perhaps thirty seconds, until he felt the tongue of the lock slide uneasily back. It was not a completely pro job—Reed had learned the art from a retired shop-breaker—because professionals tried not to leave tell-tale scratches which would identify the picks, which were worth up to a hundred pounds each. He eased the door open and disappeared inside.

Using a pencil torch, Reed plodded up the stairs and into the bathroom. The bath swung out on its rollers and Reed opened the concealed cache. In it was a cardboard container, casually fastened with tape which he pressed back with a thumb nail. Inside were neat packets of banknotes. He peeled one, for five pounds, from its sisters and rubbed it first against his cheek before shining the torch on its opaque surface. Genuine, thought Reed, beautiful genuine lolly. He sat on the top stair in darkness, watching the chink of light under the door below. You never knew how people would react so he placed his short length of lead piping in his suit breast pocket. After three-quarters of an hour the muffled sounds from below had given way to silence and Reed got stiffly to his feet. He wished to God he had a drink in his hand instead of the bit of lead piping.

There was one dim light on in the saloon bar and Joe Pollick was having his final for the day, a large green Chartreuse. Mrs. Crippen had mentioned that it was one of his few luxuries and seemed astonished that it was not a matter of general knowledge.

"I'd better pay for my own," said Reed, putting down a pound note with his left hand, and thinking as he watched Pollick straighten how at this moment they always possessed a certain calmness, sometimes short lived, just as the ruined, broken bull stared at the matador before the sword went in.

"A double Scotch, Sergeant?"

"Sounds nice."

Pollick poured, his hand steady, and added ice. "This is on me." He pushed the note back.

"You've got a few thousand gallons' worth of lolly in the loo upstairs."

"I prefer the very short ones late at night," said Pollick, sipping.

"I should have spotted that early," said Reed. "And putting something back in a place that has already been searched was a brilliant trick, and I say *was* because it is in the training manuals. If I had not checked, somebody would have taken a routine look in a couple of days' time."

"I didn't know . . ."

"How could you, not being a criminal or a cop? But you knew that Alwyn was a fence and that he had the money cached there!"

"He thought I was a robot. Eff him, all charm and brilliantine. An officer and a gentleman. Eff him. He used to stand me a farewell drink of Chartreuse when he was here after closing. When he was out I took it. I was a doormat, so were we all . . . he always took the income tax off me pay though a lot of governors don't. A rotten bastard, that's what he was."

"So you were pouring out the grog and he was bending over talking when you bashed his skull in. It worried me from the beginning. The outside door must have been locked next morning, or you would have mentioned it. Alwyn could not have locked it from the inside. I did think somebody might have kept their nerve and stayed all night until you opened up, saw the corpse and ran for a copper, but it gave me an uneasy itch."

Pollick drained the glass and poured another.

"Don't get tight, Joe, for your own good." Reed stepped a few inches back from the counter.

"I'm beyond bein' tight. I'm at the other side of the bridge. You get the trembles going over it, but then drink don't hurt you at all. It's like water." His eyes were ringed with red.

"I suppose your motive was being into the bookies for two hundred quid. They were putting it into the hands of a collector."

"There was no trouble." Pollick swayed a little. "I told them I'd pay—I've got an insurance policy coming due—but they turned on the blusterous side, so I told them to go to hell. But I'd have settled in my own good time. Eff the lot of 'em."

"Then why did you do it?"

"I knew Peter Pipchin," said Pollick. "A funny little bloke I met years back when I was working in Lambeth. He had a fiddle, o' course, but he was a quiet sort of fellow and did me a couple of turns when I needed them. He rang me up at home about seven in the morning. The phone's on the landing outside my room. Little Pete was going to nip in just before we closed at night and have a word with the Gaffer after the mugs had departed. Let me see, what was I saying? Ah, Peter was a gutsy feller, though he hadn't got no muscles, like. But he was persistent and if you got him on your tail it was like a poodle hanging on to a big dog's arse.

He'd stick there through thick and thin like wet tar on your shoes. Pete didn't trust Alwyn, who was smooth as lardy cake on top and broken bottles underneath, not that it showed much unless you watched him close. As far as I cottoned on, Pipchin had a message for Alwyn which weren't a pleasant one by a long chalk and little Peter had a rare sense about trouble . . . I remember him suddenly drinking up in a pub where I worked in North London. There was a group in the corner on the Scotch and discussion and the guv'nor had tipped me the wink to serve them slowly. Five minutes later one of them whips out a shiv and sticks it in the throat of the cove opposite him. There were other times . . ." Joe Pollick brooded and topped his glass.

"Steady," warned Reed.

"I don't care a stuff for anyone and if you don't want to listen you know where to go and pull the chain on yourself . . . I told Pete I'd put me coat on as if going, but instead nip into the storeroom off the bottle department. If things got tough he could yell out. I couldn't hear them talking and he didn't yell. I reckon it was all of twenty minutes and I was damned if I knew what to do. Then I heard breathing. I had me ear to the big, old keyhole, but substituted an eye." Pollick reached up and felt one as if to make sure it was there. "The light was on, because we use a master switch which automatically turns everything off before we go out the front door. Alwyn had little Pete slung over his shoulder like a sack of taters. I tell you I didn't like the look on Alwyn's face. All of a sudden I felt, like I'd been bitten, just what a vicious killer he was underneath, not that I think he would have had the guts to tackle a good big 'un, but a small chap or a woman and he would be in his element. Have another."

As Pollick poured the whisky Reed thought of Mrs. Gaukroger, a woman with a father fixation. She might well have liked a man such as Alwyn. Probably Pipchin had enraged Alwyn.

"He opened the trap," said Pollick, "and took the corpse

down. No doubt about it being a corpse, the way the head lolled down. I didn't know what to do. Alwyn had good ears and the front door makes a noise when you open it, perhaps intentional, I dunno. A scraping noise . . ." He was becoming obsessed with alcoholic addiction to petty detail. "As I say that might be on purpose. An honest battler don't know what *they* get up to nowadays."

"Too true." Reed tried to make it soothing. Rain had started to beat against the bar's outside windows.

"I reckoned that he might have got me before I got into the street. It was ice-cold outside and there would've been nobody about." He licked a globule of spirit off his upper lip. "Not a livin', forsaken soul about. In the fillums there's always the friendly copper loomin' out of the night, but not here, not in January. I thought fast and nipped back into the Saloon, fair shivering until 'e came back in with a nasty, peaceful look on his chops. 'I thought you had gone, Joe', he says, casual. I managed to tell him there had been a complaint about the radiators leaking in the dining-room and I had nipped in to have a look, but I sensed I hadn't fooled him none. 'You haven't 'ad your final snort, Joe', he said and went behind the bar. He got down the Chartreuse and smiled at me, the bugger, *smiled at me* as God's my flaming witness. It came into my head what my final snort might be, but I pretended not to be looking.

"I'd heard him talk to a few mates about the unarmed-combat stunts they were taught, and from the corner of my eye I saw his hand flatten and go back. They chop you under the ear 'ole and you're out to it like a side of beef. I put my head down, grabbed the Chartreuse bottle and bashed him over the head with it. I hit harder than I meant. His brains came out, a nasty sight which fair turned me stomach."

"Everybody hits harder than they mean to, Joe," said Reed softly. "And then what?"

"I went home, having my own set of keys I locked the door behind me."

"Your silly mistake, Joe, but you did more than that. You

took the pile of notes out of the hidey-hole in the bathroom and put the Chartreuse bottle in its place. That was silly, because it was quite natural for anybody's prints to be on the bottle if they worked here. And you took the loot home."

"Alwyn had a couple of those bags you get from the airlines."

"And you knew exactly where it was, under the bath!"

"You get to know when a man's got something hidden. This side of the bar what the hell is there but watching people? What they say don't mean anything, but their faces mean a lot. A lot of times Alwyn wasn't here; he left it to me and if a man had anything to hide of recent months it was him. Always fidgeting and nipping up the stairs to his private flat. Servants, animals, that's how they treat us," a boozy tear oozed on to Pollick's cheek. Reed noticed with clinical interest that it was green—over-indulgence in liqueurs did that to you. He had once met a man who sweated greenly after a bottle of crème de menthe. He estimated that in ten minutes Pollick would fall over.

"I got curiosity like everyone," snuffled Pollick.

"Don't come climbing on to my bosom," said Reed, taking another whisky, "because I'm not wasting my time sweating it out in court waiting to be called as a witness. Find another pair of tits to weep on, pally."

"You won't arrest me?" There was consternation in Pollick's voice.

"This is just a friendly talk, Joe. I'm going home in a minute. Arresting you would get me no promotion, just a lot of blooming paper-work."

Shock caused Pollick to surface again. His tearful eyes focused. "I could take the money and run."

"How would you know how to fence hot money? And the boys, Joe, the nice boys that will gouge you to death for as little as a hundred nicker. They know the lolly is around and they are hanging round the place like bees round a honeypot. I wouldn't mind betting that a couple of cars are parked in the street waiting. Try walking home with the loot."

"What will I do, mister?" Joe's voice crept from a grave.

"Lock the door behind me, finish the bottle and pass out. In the morning get a solicitor, but tell the truth, pally, or you'll spend the rest of your days on boiled bacon."

"Have one with me, sir, I couldn't drink alone."

Reed smiled and walked to the front door, slamming it behind him.

He felt bilious as he turned up his collar against the steady rain. There would be no cab inside two miles.

Being an Englishman he thought vaguely that tomorrow might be sunny.